DUTY AND DESIRE

DUTY AND DESIRE
MILITARY EROTIC ROMANCE

EDITED BY
KRISTINA WRIGHT

FOREWORD BY
CAT JOHNSON

CLEIS
PRESS

Published in the United States by Cleis Press, Inc., 2246 Sixth Street, Berkeley, California 94710.

Printed in the United States.
Cover design: Scott Idleman/Blink
Cover photograph: Blend Images/John Fedele
Text design: Frank Wiedemann
First Edition.
10 9 8 7 6 5 4 3 2 1

Trade paper ISBN: 978-1-57344-823-9
E-book ISBN: 978-1-57344-837-6

Contents

FOREWORD

When I was asked to write the foreword for *Duty and Desire: Military Erotic Romance*, I thought first about focusing on how hot I find a man—or men—in uniform. It's one of the main reasons I've been writing in the genre since 2006. But as I thought about it, I realized my dedication to the genre is about so much more than sex appeal. It goes far deeper than fantasizing about hard bodies in heart-stopping uniforms.

It's a delicate dance we authors do when writing about men and women in uniform. Balancing fantasy and reality, taking the cold hardness of war and wrapping it in fiction and romance. Softening the edges enough to make it palatable and entertaining because that is the business we're in, after all. We attempt to do all of that while still honoring the small and large sacrifices selflessly made by our troops, both past and present. They endure heat and cold, bad food and worse living conditions. Then there are the larger sacrifices—being separated from loved ones for extended periods of time. Missing huge chunks of life at home. And, of course, there are the injuries and casualties that are an unavoidable part of war.

It's not an easy task, this balancing act. We know there are readers who live with the fear and sacrifice daily and they need a brief escape, even if only for the few hours they can lose themselves in our books. But at the same time, we can't ignore the realities completely. We need to be aware of and acknowledge it all—the loneliness, the boredom, the hope, the fear. The mundane things that take on larger meaning while being separated from loved ones. Something as seemingly small as mail call is so important for the deployed—bringing disappointment for those who receive nothing, while at the same time delivering glee to those who get a small piece of home.

I know the responsibility of portraying all of that. Delicately weaving the threads within an erotic tale, a romance with a happy ending, is a weight on my shoulders. It's a responsibility I feel, as I know my fellow authors do too, every time I undertake writing a new military-themed story.

How do we do it? How do we write stories that balance both light and dark? Entertain as well as enlighten? We show the good, as well as the bad. Is there good in war? Yes. There is the camaraderie that those who have served know so well, and those of us who have not may never fully appreciate. The knowledge that one soldier would willingly die for the man to his right, just as the soldier to his left would willingly die for him. But there's so much more as well. The grabbing life with both hands and living it to the fullest because they know more than most how fleeting it can be. Emotions run high. Love comes fast and hard. And yes, sex too—because what can possibly make us feel more alive than that most intimate of all connections with another human being?

That living life to the fullest is why I undertook writing in this genre, even if it can be daunting. The sheer intensity of how those in uniform live and love is transfixing. We want to feel it too, to share in that intensity. We want to love as deeply. Feel as strongly. We want to fall in love with that alpha male willing to kill or die to protect us, just as we want to make him fall in love with us. We want to be the one who makes him fight to live another day. We want to be on the receiving end of all that intensity. It's why military stories and the heroes they feature are inherently passionate, intense, sexy and inspiring. And yes, there are the uniforms as well, so sexy when drawn tight over the hard bodies. The cropped hair and the intense stare. The rough exterior hiding the smoldering inside. Those who don a uniform daily and fight to protect us at home can make any heart beat faster.

I feel confident I can speak for all the authors featured in this book, whether the story they penned is modern or historical, lighthearted and sexy or intensely dark. If we can make you feel the emotions we strive to convey, we've done our job. We've honored those in uniform we're privileged to write about. And hopefully at the same time we've provided, just for a little while, an escape into that world.

Thank you for taking the journey with us.

Cat Johnson

INTRODUCTION: BEYOND THE UNIFORM

It was my husband Jay's first deployment as a naval officer. After ten years as an enlisted sailor, he'd finished his bachelor's degree and received his commission. The pier was crowded with sailors and civilian family members saying good-bye. The atmosphere was festive even though the occasion was sad. I scanned the pier looking for Jay amid the chaos. It took less than one minute to pick him out of the sea of summer white uniforms. "There he is!" The friend who was with me said, "How did you know it was him? They all look alike!"

Jay was hours from leaving on a six-month deployment—one of several we have been through in our years together—so I was more interested in catching up to him than I was in explaining why I recognized him in a crowd of officers dressed just like him. But here's the answer: when you look beyond the uniform, it's easy to find the person you love. I wasn't looking for a uniform or an insignia, I was looking for my sailor. And I found him easily by the way he carried himself. It was in the tilt of his head, the swagger in his step and the ramrod straight posture of a man preparing for duty.

Soldiers and sailors and their brethren are romantic heroes on the page because they embody those qualities we love and want in a partner—honor, integrity, loyalty, selflessness, courage. The fact that they also look hot in uniform is just an added bonus. But it's not the uniform that makes the man—it's the man (or woman) who makes the uniform. My sailor is *my* sailor, in or out of uniform, and he lives by the same sense of honor whether he's on a ship in the middle of the Mediterranean Ocean or lying on the couch with our two little boys. He lives his life with the same passion and enthusiasm he serves his country with, and it's those qualities that make him not only a good naval officer—but a good husband and father.

For this anthology, I wanted to go beyond the uniform and discover the men and women who dedicate their lives—or at least part of their lives—to the service of their country. I discovered stories that explored the many layers of military experience, from the excitement of special operations to the turmoil of war, the joy of reunions to the poignancy of loss. Whether it was the lighthearted side of lust on liberty or the love that lasts long after a soldier is discharged, the authors in *Duty and Desire* did *their* literary duty in creating characters who live and love in and out of uniform. Regardless of length of service, the military changes a person forever—and these stories reflect that. Here you will find passion that overcomes obstacles and limitations, couples who are willing to do anything to be together and love that lasts come hell or high water.

Whether you have served in the military, loved someone who has or simply admired those who do, these stories are for you, dear reader. I hope they touch your heart and inspire delicious patriotic fantasies. All is fair in love and war, but in *Duty and Desire*, love wins. Love *always* wins.

Kristina Wright
In love in Hampton Roads, Virginia

THE LONG
RIDE HOME

Delilah Devlin

White-hot sun beat down on the tops of our helmets. Sweat pooled between our shoulder blades and dampened the necks of our T-shirts. But it was a hot, humid East Texas heat, unlike what we'd endured for the past eleven months, and none of us standing in formation really minded. We were home.

I watched sweat trickle down the side of one particular soldier's neck as he stood in the row in front of me and thought, not for the first time, that I'd like the chance to lick it away.

Not that Staff Sergeant Mason Haddox had a clue how I felt. We'd been part of the same platoon—played volleyball and shot hoops, driven trucks over long, barely paved expanses of desert and mountains, and cleaned our weapons, side by side, but he hadn't seen me as anything but another private who needed looking after.

And yet, his tall, muscled frame, black close-cropped hair and wintry blue eyes had made quite an impression on me. I'd lusted after him since the first time he'd shown up drill weekend, a month before we'd deployed. His steadfast calm during the most nightmarish day of my life had only cemented his attraction.

My nose started to itch, and I wrinkled it, hoping formation would break soon so I could scratch it. My feet were roasting in the boots sticking to the black pavement.

True to his word, our commander kept his speech short. A good thing, since SSG Haddox fidgeted, hands tightening and easing, swaying slightly on his feet as though waiting to spring into action. I knew he scanned the crowd seated in the bleachers from the corners of his eyes, hoping she'd show, that she'd changed her mind. I'd looked too and knew she wasn't there—and wouldn't be coming. I felt bad for him but was also secretly hopeful that he'd be ready to let go, that he wouldn't do something stupid now that we were back.

Just a month before we began preparations for our unit's return from Afghanistan, Haddox had gotten the Dear John letter from his girlfriend, informing him that she'd moved his belongings from their apartment into a storage unit. She'd included two keys taped to the page—one for the storage unit and one to his Mustang. She'd said she was sorry, but had he really expected her to wait all those months?

Had I been in her shoes, I would have. But then, I knew what it felt like to be so far from home that Skype and email couldn't fill the loneliness. I'd survived it once. However, my husband's second tour had severed our connection—that and the emails I'd discovered when I'd hacked his Gmail account. Ones he'd sent to a female corporal stationed in another province who was planning a little R&R rendezvous. As quick as that, my love for him dried up like a closed tap. I'd forwarded the email to my account, then sent it to him along with a request for a divorce.

So I knew what Haddox felt. The searing betrayal. The anger.

Maybe she'd been a decent person, but personally, I consigned her to hell. The worst thing the person at home could do to a deployed soldier was abandon him when he was too far away to do a damn thing about it.

I hoped he didn't plan to go find her now.

"Company, attention!"

I snapped into position.

"Dismissed."

Cheers from our unit and from the family and friends who filled the armory motor pool rang in the late-afternoon air. Haddox stomped away, not bothering to share a word with anyone.

My sister waved and made her way through the throng spilling from the bleachers, a wide smile splitting her face. I gave her an answering smile, but couldn't help darting a glance to watch that broad set of shoulders move toward the open motor pool gates—the only space large enough to hold the formation and the guests who'd come to welcome the reserve unit home.

The buses that had delivered us from the airport were pulling away. Most of the soldiers and their friends and family were heading inside the armory for the welcome home celebration, but Haddox was heading toward the parking lot.

I gave my sister a quick hug. "Go say hi to Shelby—he's got it bad for you."

She laughed and blushed. "Where are you goin'?" Then her gaze followed mine. "Seriously? I thought you said he was an asshole."

"He grows on you. I'm sorry. I have to go."

She gave me a smile and hitched her purse over her shoulder. "Don't worry about me. But you better call."

"Tell Shelby to grab my gear!" I said before I took off.

Haddox was already dropping his duffel bag into the trunk

of a car—an older model black Mustang. I halted beside him, trying to figure out what I could say to keep him from driving away.

"You forget something, PFC Hollister?" he asked, glancing at me as he slammed down the trunk lid.

"Megan," I said, suddenly breathless. "Thought you might like some company."

His gaze narrowed. "Did you, now? I'm gonna blow the carbon out of the exhaust. The ride's gonna be bumpy."

"I don't want to get in the way—if you have plans."

He snorted. "No plans. Don't even have a place to sleep. Didn't your sister come to pick you up?"

"Yeah, but she's all right with me leavin'."

This time, his mouth twisted into something between a smile and a snarl. "Shelby?"

"Yeah. You know they've been writing each other."

His gaze trailed straight down my body, then up again. "Get in."

I strode quickly to the passenger door, opened it and slipped into the bucket seat. Then I tossed my hat in the backseat and began unbuttoning my ACU-camouflaged jacket.

He slid in beside me, one dark brow lifted, but he didn't say a thing when I threw it into the back and sat in my sweat-damp shirt in the musty car.

"Better roll down the windows." Then he said a little prayer under his breath and turned the key in the ignition. I buckled my seat belt. The engine rumbled into life. With a quick, tight grin, he jerked the stick into reverse and then punched it forward, and we rolled out onto the street, heading west rather than east into town.

Hot wind whipped through the interior of the car, dispelling the musty air and tugging at my blond hair, which was looped into a clip at the back of my head. I reached back and released it, then laughed as the Mustang roared.

Glancing toward Haddox, I noted the hard edge of his jaw, the hand wrapped so tight around the steering wheel, the tensed muscles in his forearm. I didn't have to crawl inside his head to know he didn't want me there, but I was.

Maybe I could help him out a bit. And maybe he'd see me as more than a fellow soldier who'd shared the bench seat of a deuce-and-a-half truck a time or two. One I'd been driving when he'd had to talk me through a hail of gunfire when our transport convoy had come under attack.

I unbuckled my belt, ignoring his deep frown. I turned in the seat and reached for the buttons of his jacket, flicking them open, then parting each side.

He didn't say a thing, but his nostrils flared and his jaw tightened.

I gripped the front of his T-shirt, bunched it in my hand, and tugged it from his ACU trousers.

His stomach jumped, and he sucked it in, making just enough room for me to get my fingers behind the waistband as I unbuckled, unbuttoned and tugged down the zip.

"Dammit, Hollister," he said, his voice rough as gravel. "You're gonna get us both killed."

"Not if you keep your eyes on the road," I said, tilting up my chin. Then I leaned over his lap, folded down the elastic band of his boxer briefs and pulled his cock upright.

"Fuck." The car bolted forward. I had a glimpse of the long, black ribbon of highway, then turned my attention to his thickening cock.

I fingered the curve of the satin-soft cap. "I never said thanks for saving my ass."

"I didn't expect it."

"I know. But it meant a lot, knowing you had faith I wouldn't freak."

"I recall shouting at you, calling you a pansy-assed waitress."

"Which I was, and will be again." I leaned toward him, brushing my breasts against his firm upper arms. "You made me mad enough to want to kill you."

"Which I take it turned you on?"

"Not right then. But later. Every time I heard you shout, I creamed."

His eyelids dipped down and he shot me a searing glance. "My dick's out. Gonna do something with it, or were you just curious, Hollister?"

"I've seen it before—at the showers, when Specialist Shelby whipped off your towel."

He grunted. "Most of the camp saw me stomp back to the tent in my birthday suit. Not my finest moment."

"It was one of the highlights of the tour for me."

"Better get busy or put it back."

I winked. "Yes, Sarge. I'm pretty good at followin' orders."

His chuckle was low and dirty, but his expression had softened a fraction. He wasn't thinking about the bitch who'd dumped him in a letter now.

Sure I had his full attention, I bent, slipping a hand inside his briefs to fondle his balls while I wet the tip of his cock with long drags of my tongue. Then I dove deeper, taking him into my mouth, suctioning to pull him deeper and stroking my tongue along the sides of his shaft.

He hardened quickly inside my mouth, expanding, stretching, veins rising against the steely shaft. I bobbed over his lap, quietly at first, but soon couldn't help the little slurping sounds I made as my mouth watered, coating him. His balls tightened, pulling closer to his groin, and I tugged them gently until he widened his thighs and melted against the seat.

I moaned around him, then shifted to get my knees under me on the seat. I pulled my hand from his underwear and gripped the edge of the dash and his shoulder for better leverage, then dove again and again, taking him deep into my throat, lunging faster and faster.

His belly jumped, the engine growled—then fingers dug into my scalp and tugged my head from his lap. "Get your pants off."

With my heart beating hard against my chest, I struggled with my boots, flipping them over the seat, and then tossed back my pants. The bikinis I dropped to the floorboard—in case I needed them in a hurry.

Haddox pulled the car onto the shoulder of the road, slid back his seat, then urged me over his lap. "This what you were after?"

I reached between us and set the tip of his cock at the entrance of my vagina. "I owe you."

"You don't owe me a damn thing." His hands gripped each side of my hips and held me still. "Why me? Why now?"

"We're stateside. Not breakin' any laws."

"Beg your pardon, but I can think of a few." He leaned toward me and rooted through my T-shirt until his mouth latched onto a nipple. He bit it. "First stateside fuck? Not buying it." He nipped it again, harder.

I gasped and dug my fingers into his close-cropped hair. "I want you, Haddox."

"Mason. We're gonna fuck—call me Mason."

"Mason, I want you. Have for the longest, but you had a girl. I wouldn't do that to another woman. Not when she couldn't be there to fight for you."

He released my breast. "You divorced your husband when he was deployed."

"He cheated."

He grunted, centered me again and slid me down his cock, his fingers biting into my hips as he controlled the slow glide. "Man was a damn fool."

"It happens. We were apart too damn long."

"I waited."

"So did I. But I'm not bitter." I squeezed my pussy around him. "Dammit, let me move."

His grip eased, and his hands slid up the inside of my shirt and under my bra. His fingers were hard but caressed me gently, massaging me as I began to move.

"When did it get dark?" I murmured, clutching his shoulders. Despite the tight confines and the steering wheel rubbing my back, I rose and fell, slowly at first, then faster, watching the last glimmer of the setting sun as it burned against the horizon.

His breaths deepened. He pinched my nipples and pulled them, letting them go, then pulled them again. Excitement cramped my belly, slicked my channel and his dick.

His eyelids dipped, and he shoved up my shirt to watch as he continued to torture my breasts. The tips extended, and he twirled them between his fingers.

I plunged down his cock again. "Mason," I gasped.

"Do you know what I'm gonna do to you first motel we find?"

"Jesus, what?" I said, lunging down and settling against him to rub my clit against his pelvic bone and wiry curls.

"Tie you to it. Then lick you from your toes to your tits and back down. Might leave a mark or two along the way."

I smiled. "Haven't had a hickey since high school."

"Ever been spanked?"

I tilted my head. "Wanna use your belt on me?"

"Fabric doesn't sting as much as leather. Will that be enough for you, wildcat?"

I laughed. "Think so. And I like it doggie-style. Rattle the bed when you fuck me."

"I can manage that. If we can get food delivered, I might not want to leave the bed for a week."

I groaned. "Seems just about long enough."

"To make up for no sex for a year?"

"To get to know you."

Mason blew out a deep breath, then pushed back my hair. "You know me, Megan," he whispered. "You knew I couldn't be alone today."

"Then maybe it'll be long enough for you to know me."

"Oh, I know you. I called you a wimp when you were scared. Got you riled enough to gun it and run that truck through the barricade. I wanted to kiss you when we made it back to camp."

His cock crowded through swollen tissue. I bit my bottom lip as I savored the stretch. "Really?"

"Yeah, but Marla was still part of my life, or so I thought."

I wrinkled my nose. "And it would've been breakin' the rules."

"That too." He cleared his throat. "Think we might finish this up before some cop comes drivin' by and arrests both our naked asses?"

"Don'tcha think he'd give two soldiers home from war a break?"

"Maybe, but I'm not in the mood to have to flash him my own badge, and I don't want anyone seein' your ass but me."

I rose and fell, squeezing my pussy hard, making double damn sure he knew I wasn't going to rush a minute of my first

Mason-induced orgasm. "When we wrap up this week in bed, will I see you again?"

"Think I need a war to know I need this—and you?"

"A girl likes to know she's more than a fuck, Mason."

"Baby, I do believe you're gonna be my favorite fuck."

I rammed down his cock and held still, glaring daggers at his sly smile.

His gaze held mine as he fit two fingers into the top of my folds and rubbed my clit, toggling back and forth.

My whole body shivered, and I gave a whimper.

"Can't resist it, can you? Gonna do what I ask, baby? Gonna come for me now?"

I closed my eyes and rocked forward and back, grinding against him, building friction, getting wetter and wetter. When he leaned toward me and kissed my mouth, I cried out and burrowed my tongue into his mouth, tasting him fully for the first time as waves of hot and cold pleasure rippled through me.

I vibrated on his cock, squeezing, releasing, and then his thighs tensed beneath me, and he shoved up then down, tunneling deeper, stroking in and out until, at last, he shuddered and his whole body tightened. Come spurted deep inside me, and I gave quick thanks to the fact I was still on the pill. Neither of us was ready for complications.

His mouth softened beneath mine, and he rubbed his lips on mine before pulling back. "Do something for me?"

"I already did," I murmured.

"Stay naked. I like the idea of you slickin' up the leather while I drive."

I grinned and eased slowly off his cock. While he tucked himself back into his pants and changed gears to pull out onto the highway, I sat beside him, my thighs slightly parted to let them dry.

He placed a hand between my legs, and two fingers slipped into my pussy. "Any complaints?" he asked, his smile digging a dimple into one cheek.

I flipped back my hair, snuggled my back into the leather and closed my eyes. "I'll let you know, soldier." So what if I didn't have a toothbrush or a change of clothes? The fingers gliding through my folds were determined and sparking a second coming that had me sliding lower in my seat. I trusted him. He knew me. It was enough for now. We'd come home and neither of us wanted to be alone.

The scrubby live oaks and cedar trees dotting the rugged hills blurred as my eyelids fell. I smiled, thinking about how I must look—tanned legs spread, T-shirt bundled under my breasts.

His thumb rasped my swollen clit. I peeked at him. His face was turned away, but he was smiling too, and looking like a man well-satisfied with how things had gone down.

"Are you sorry it's me?" I asked, then instantly regretted it. I didn't want to sound needy.

His eyes reflected the lights from the dash when he shot me a quick glare. "I was pissed she didn't bother to show, but when you jumped into my car, I realized I didn't even know what color her eyes were." He gave a snort. "Yours, sweetheart, are gold-brown with little green flecks. I've noticed things about your from the very start. If I hadn't wanted you in this car, I'd have patted your butt and sent you on your way."

I faced forward again, satisfied that was probably the most romantic thing the man might ever tell me. I cupped my hand over the one still playing between my thighs and settled in for the long ride.

NIGHT WITCH

Connie Wilkins

Far away someone played the balalaika.

Darkness still gripped Yelena, slashed by searchlights and bursts of antiaircraft fire. Over and over she glided silently, engine cut, the only warning for the German defenses the whistling of the wind through the biplane's wing struts—until Yevgeniya in the navigator's cockpit released the bombs. Over and over; the silent approach, the bombs dropping, exploding, then the side-slipping her plane out of the searchlight beams and restarting the engine—but never the flight back to their base. Never escape.

Yet now there was balalaika music. A simple tune, simply played, achingly sweet. The notes tugged at her heart, her mind, and led her at last out of darkness.

At first all she saw was the fire in the hearth. Then the subtle movement of fingers plucking the balalaika's strings caught her eye. Her gaze moved up along a muscular forearm to the shirt-sleeve rolled tightly across the bicep, and onward to the dark head bowed over the instrument. He sat near the hearth on a low stool, and the firelight glinted on streaks of silver in his hair; but that hand, that arm, were not those of an old man.

A dream, of course, but much more pleasant than the dark one. Often at an encampment when they could snatch some sleep she had dreamed of a small farm cottage, a hearth and perhaps even a man in the background, though visions of a simple piece of rye bread and a bowl of hot barley soup had ranked higher. Some of the girls in the all-women's regiment talked on and on about men, while others, like Yevgeniya...

"Yevgeniya!" Yelena struggled to sit in spite of a throbbing pain in her head. The balalaika music ceased abruptly. But the room, the fire, the man calmly rolling his shirtsleeves back down and lighting a lamp with a brand from the fire were still there. Not a dream, then.

Now she remembered Yevgeniya calling, "Lena! Lenotchka! Can you get free?" while her hands tugged so frantically that Yelena had blacked out from the pain.

"Yevgeniya?" She fought back panic. More memories came; the blasted wing, the plane plunging and shuddering as she struggled to keep in the air long enough to safely cross into Russian-held territory.

"Your navigator survived the crash with only a few cuts and bruises." He took up a walking stick that had leaned against the chimney and made his way slowly toward her. An old man after all? The lamp showed a long scar across his cheek beside his left ear, disappearing under his collar. A good face, with strong bones, lined by pain and stress rather than age. Not old, but wounded, which explained why he could be here instead of in the army with every Russian male fit to fight.

He set the lamp on a wooden table and pulled a chair up beside the couch where she lay. "She saw my light on the hillside and came to me for help, with her handgun ready in case I should need persuading. Such a forceful girl! The Germans are wrong to call your bomber crews 'Night Witches.' That one is more like an avenging Valkyrie."

Yelena smiled at that, but asked, "Where is she now?" She felt for the handgun that should be in her flight suit pocket, and realized suddenly that she lay all but naked under a soft woolen blanket.

"Your weapon is beside your pillow."

The hint of amusement in his voice dispelled her sudden fear. She restrained herself from groping for the gun.

"Once convinced that I would not eat you, she went to find the nearest Russian troops and then to make her way to your airfield. She will send help for you if she can. She assured me, though, that you would understand her first duty is to get back into the air and drop more bombs on the invaders."

"So it is," Yelena said. "And mine as well."

"Then mine must be to make sure you're fit to travel and to fly. No bones broken, but your leg was badly bruised by the fuel tank that trapped you in the cockpit, and yesterday your head had a lump as big as a goose egg." He reached out and gently lifted the russet hair away from her temple. "Tonight I think we have only a common hen's egg to deal with."

Yelena's hand went to her wound. She flinched at the soreness. There was indeed a lump, and a short gash already scabbing over. She must have bled a great deal. But... "Yesterday? How long have I been here? And how long has Yevgeniya been gone?"

"She was off within a quarter of an hour after we brought you here." He said it very casually, but Yelena knew he understood what she was thinking. This man had not only rescued her, even wounded as he was, but had cared for her unconscious body for at least a day and a night.

The thought of his strong hands cleaning away the blood, removing her clothing, doing for her whatever else had been necessary, did not trouble her as much as it should have. She felt a traitorous flush rise from her chest to her cheeks, but kept her voice steady. "Then I thank you for your care of me."

"You would do the same for any fellow soldier of the Rodina."

It was true, though something in his eyes made Yelena hope that she was not just any fellow soldier to him. It could hardly matter, though, since she must indeed return to flying, and her chances of survival were less even than for foot soldiers in the Russian Army.

The army. She struggled again to sit up, and managed it with his right arm around her shoulders. "Are we still behind our own lines?"

"The German guns have been coming closer. One more day, perhaps."

There was no need to explain the danger. If the Germans found the remains of her mangled Po-2 biplane, their search for survivors would be unrelenting. No "Night Witch" had yet been captured; they had each been given handguns to assure that none ever would. Better to die that way.

She clutched at his hand. His fingers tightened around hers. "I must get back on my feet. What should I call you?" It felt strange that she did not already know.

"Arkady is my name. But...wait while I find something for you to wear." He rose and turned away so quickly that she guessed he was trying to spare her embarrassment. Or, she found herself hoping, trying to keep from staring as intently as he wished.

How had she forgotten her undressed state? Her fur-lined flight suit and wool uniform and ill-fitting army-issue undergarments were gone completely, and all that covered her was a man's cotton undershirt that might have covered her to the hips if her movements hadn't bunched it higher. Just the thought of his gaze on her body made her tightened nipples show clearly through thin fabric. "What has become of my own clothing?" she called after him, more to distract herself than out of curiosity.

"Burned. And then buried. The fuel tank had leaked onto you, and there was so much blood...and to keep them here was too dangerous."

Of course. Yelena pulled the blanket back over her lap. This was no time for... Or perhaps it was. War topples all conventions. She was no virgin, after all. How could one deny a childhood friend going off to fight and likely never to come back? All the girls in her village had done their part. It was not until a year later that she had discovered how much more she could do for her country, when the famous aviator Marina Raskova persuaded Comrade Stalin to let her form female air regiments, with women trained in the aeroclubs so popular across the country in the last decade. Surely by now, after more than 800 bombing missions, she deserved some pleasures of her own choosing.

Arkady could be seen through an open door rummaging through a chest at the foot of a wide bed. When he returned he brought a nightrobe of fine embroidered wool. "I don't suppose my grandmother ever actually wore this after her wedding night, only saved it with her bridal clothes and other treasures."

"Lovely," Yelena said sincerely. "I hope she wouldn't mind letting me use it."

"She would call you a heroine of the Motherland, and be honored," he said gravely, and after that she couldn't refuse.

When she sat decently clothed at the edge of the couch, he

helped her stand erect. The bruised leg felt as though it might give way, and her head began to pound. Her first steps were unsteady, but motion strengthened her, and she walked on her own to the haven of a chair on the far side of the table.

"Good! That deserves a reward." Arkady took two bowls from a shelf and limped without his stick toward the iron cookstove beside the chimney. Only then did Yelena realize that the aroma of barley soup had been teasing at her subconscious mind. In dreams it had always come first, but now the man—and the danger—had distracted her. Even his movements, stooping to add wood to the fire, preoccupied her, and she wondered how far down past his shirt and into his loose farmer's trousers his scar extended.

They shared the soup, thick with carrots and onion and bits of chicken, and slices of rye bread far enough past fresh to be ideal for dipping into the broth. Yelena was suddenly so hungry that she ate much too fast and let a bite of soup-sodden bread slide down her chin. Arkady laughed, and she grinned widely, until she saw him wince and touch the scar on his face.

"Does it hurt?" She wished she dared reach out to soothe him.

"No, just...pulls a bit if I laugh, although I can't remember the last time I did that. Does anyone laugh in these times?"

"One must laugh, to prove to fate that you are alive!" This time Yelena did reach across the table to touch his face, and, after a tiny flinch, Arkady did not pull away. "You should do it as exercise, to stretch the scar tissue. And rub it with the ointment my grandmother used to make with goose grease and herbs." She ran a finger very lightly down his wounded cheek and felt a tremor he could not suppress. She did not think pain was its cause. When her hand reached his throat he pulled it gently away, but did not let it go.

"My grandmother never kept geese," he said, "but she had her own home remedies." His tone was light, though the darkened eyes fixed on hers were saying something else entirely. "Her chickens and sheep are still here, in my care, while she has gone to live in a safer area with my cousins."

"I expect chicken fat would do. Or lanolin from the sheep's wool." Yelena too was matter-of-fact, while in her imagination she rubbed ointment all along his wounds however far beneath his clothing they extended. "Proper massaging can work wonders for stiffened scars."

Arkady dropped her hand and stood abruptly. "You had better watch out, Lenotchka, or I will decide you make an even better nurse than pilot, and keep you here."

"I am a *very* good pilot, Arkasha," Yelena said teasingly. Did he even realize that he had used the intimate form of her name, and she had responded in kind?

"I'm sure you could also be a *very* good nurse." He retreated with his walking stick to the stool by the hearth and picked up the balalaika, idly stroking its polished surface. "And if you cured me, I could go back to...to do my part for the Rodina." All the lightness left his voice. "In truth, I should go back now. I knew, when I managed to pry that fuel tank away and carried you with the Valkyrie's aid all the long way back here, that I was well enough now to do whatever must be done."

"And what..." Yelena hesitated. "How did..."

"A building fell around me." Arkady stared into the fire.

She didn't press him, and instead asked, "Is the balalaika your own, or your grandmother's?"

"My mother's. The music is all I remember of her."

So much for finding a more pleasant topic for conversation. But then he said, so quietly she could scarcely hear, "I have not played for years, but tonight I had the strangest thought that she was telling me to play the music to wake you."

"I'm very glad she did." Yelena struggled to find words to tell him how truly she meant that, but nothing came.

After a time he rose and walked to the bedroom door, body taut with the effort not to lean on his stick. "You sleep in my grandmother's bed tonight. I will keep watch out here and tend the fire."

Yelena made her way around the table. While Arkady stood at the bedroom door, she deliberately slipped out of the lovely robe, folded it neatly, and set it on the couch. Then, her back toward him, she wriggled out of the clinging undershirt. If words could not tell him of her feelings, she would find a different means.

"We will both sleep in your grandmother's bed tonight." She turned back and picked up the lamp. "She would call you a hero of the Rodina as well, and approve of some good nursing."

As she brushed past him he gripped the door frame so tightly that his knuckles showed white, and not, she thought, because of his injured leg.

The lamp went on a bedside table, and Yelena sat on the bed's feather-stuffed coverlet. "Surely," she said, "after so much death, we can have a brief taste of life. And of comfort." The quaver in her voice was both genuine and deliberate.

"Your injuries..." But he moved closer with no trace of a limp and stood looking down at her.

Yelena shrugged, knowing his gaze followed the lifting of her breasts. "And yours. Don't worry, I will be gentle."

"I will try," Arkady said, with a gleam of amusement, "but I cannot promise such a difficult thing."

"Begin with something easier." She grasped his arms and pulled herself up along his body. "Let me help you take off your clothes. Fair's fair. And I'm your nurse."

He glanced toward the lamp; this was not so easy, and she knew it. His hidden scars, those of the body at least, must be severe enough that he feared to reveal them. The flesh, however, had already revealed by its urgent thrust against hers what she needed most to know; that part of him was intact, and so eager that her own desire intensified. She pressed in even closer.

"Please, Arkasha," she murmured. Under her hands the buttons of his shirt gave way, one of them even flying off into the shadows. "Let me feel you. I have seen many wounds, even unto death. Yours are precious to me."

Arkady groaned at the stroke of her fingers on his bare chest. She touched her lips to the raised, livid streak along his left side, then kissed all along it down to the point where it descended beneath his trousers, and further yet when she had managed to unfasten those and pull his underdrawers lower. "Ointment would be best," she said, "but we must make do with what we have," and she applied her tongue to the task.

Yelena sat back down on the bed, pulled his garments all the way down to his boots and licked gently along the cruel scar that tapered off just where the tender skin of his inner thigh met even more tender flesh. He thrust his fingers into her thick russet hair and tried to pull her head to where he clearly needed it most.

Yelena stopped just short of his goal and pulled back, the bruise on her head aching from the pressure. "Come into the bed, Arkasha, between the covers. I've seen now where I must be gentlest, and where I may play at will." Her fingers traced a promise along his quite startling length before she folded down the bed's coverlet and lay back.

"Gentleness be damned!" he growled, but threw himself down beside her and pulled the covering over them both.

Yelena was on him at once, straddling his body while his

hands moved over hers in a storm of stroking and pressing and tormenting. Their mouths clung and moved against each other, each pressure speaking more than any words, until the need for even sharper sensation made her pull free. Her aching breasts and nipples claimed the attentions of his lips and tongue and teeth, and her mouth was now free to let out sighs and moans and inarticulate pleas. Meanwhile he explored her tender folds and swellings until she could bear the protracted pleasure no longer and settled herself firmly onto his searching cock. By stages she raised up and slid down as he thrust from beneath until she had taken him in completely. Their movements became a dance of lust, a give and take with no room for thought, only for need, and more need, and at last a pulsing demand that burst into a blaze of fulfillment.

When their cries diminished, Yelena thought she heard the throb of a Po-2 engine, familiar as her own heartbeat, pass by overhead on a bombing mission. While sleep claimed her, held close in Arkady's arms, she wondered fuzzily which of her friends had been piloting the plane and whether even there in the sky they had heard her cry out.

The sun was high when Yelena woke. The bed beside her was empty, and a skirt and blouse in an old-fashioned style were laid out on a chair, along with a wool shawl and shabby boots such as a farmwoman would wear. More things Arkady's grand-mother had left behind. Her handgun lay on top of the pile. She dressed quickly in spite of stiffness, some of which was really quite pleasurable, and went out into the main room, her gun in the skirt's capacious pocket.

Arkady stood by the window that looked out over the valley. Beside him was no walking stick, but a long rifle of antique design.

Yelena went to him and leaned as naturally into the quick

pressure of his arm around her waist as if they had always been together. "You have a gun," she commented unnecessarily.

"An old one. No wolf has come down from the mountains after our sheep for many years, but one never knows." He manipulated the rifle, checking its parts, making adjustments, then raised and sighted along it. Merely an exercise, but even to Yelena it was clear that his skill with guns went far beyond that of an ordinary farmer, or even foot soldier.

He saw her expression. "I was on the shooting team at the Academy of Agriculture when I studied there."

She was not deceived into taking that as the whole story. "And where were you when the building fell around you?"

There could be no more secrets between them. "In Kiev," he said. "And now there is need of me in Stalingrad. I cannot run, but I can still shoot."

A sharpshooter, sniper, picking off selected targets on city streets, through windows, in blasted buildings as shells landed around them, and a target himself. If only they could run away together!

But her own duty called as firmly as his. "I too have a gun," she said. "And now they are coming." She could see through the window where a German motorcar had emerged from a wooded area a mile away and was making its slow bumpy way along the lane.

"Shooting a man face-to-face is a different thing from dropping bombs. Especially in your dreams."

"I can do it." Yelena hoped she spoke the truth.

"You may need to, but not here. Leave right now. Our troops are directly to the east, judging by the planes overhead last night. I will persuade these invaders that you were never here."

They both knew that there was no time for her to travel across the open fields and out of sight behind the next ridge.

His plan was to kill every German in the car, sacrificing his own life if necessary, to give her a chance to get away.

"You will never persuade anyone with a nose that there was no woman in your bed last night. And why should your new bride not be with you? Can you play the simple sheepherder? If after all it comes to killing, two guns are better than one."

By now there could be no other choice. Arkady smoothed her hair over the bruise on her temple, scarcely swollen now, kissed her deeply, then went outside. When the motorcar lurched to a stop, Arkady waited, leaning heavily on his walking stick. "You have frightened my sheep!" he called in a querulous voice as soon as the interpreter opened his door, and indeed five sheep could be seen running off on the grassy hillside.

Four uniformed Germans emerged, barking questions faster than the interpreter, an ethnic German born in Russia, could handle. At last Arkady shrugged and let them file past into the house. Yelena stood stirring a pot on the stove and looking very young and frightened.

"They search for the crew of the plane that crashed down below." He came to stand beside her, moving with an exaggerated limp.

"Was it their plane?" she asked the interpreter timidly. "I only returned yesterday, and he told me of it."

"You should have obeyed me and stayed in the north with your mother," Arkady growled at her. "I told you it was too dangerous here!"

Yelena dared to show a flash of spirit. "You were glad enough that I was not with my mother last night!" She mustered a convincing blush as she looked around at the others. One of the younger Germans laughed and muttered to his comrade, who snickered and shook his head. Yelena knew little of the German language, but was quite sure she heard the word *Nachthexen*.

Night Witches. From the way the soldiers looked her over, she was very nearly sure that they had judged her too pretty to be a witch. Their officer watched her keenly with a different sort of assessment.

"And if I am not here," she went on, "who will sew on your buttons? See what a state you get into without me!" Arkady wore the shirt from the night before, when she had sent a button flying in her haste to strip him. "Who will make cheese from the sheep's milk? And rub ointment on your scars?"

It was Arkady's turn to duck his head and look embarrassed. "Tell them to look around as they please," he muttered to the interpreter. "Women pilots, did you say? If you find any, take them away! One woman is trouble enough."

More laughter, followed by a thorough search of the house and outbuildings. One young soldier emerged from the bedroom carrying the embroidered wedding nightrobe, and whispered a sly comment to his friend, but at last the group went on to search elsewhere. Yelena knew by the officer's backward glance that they would still be watched from time to time.

"Hold me," she begged Arkady, who pulled her so close that her voice was muffled against his shoulder. "They will spy on us, I'm sure."

"And what should they see but a man whose wife cannot bear to stay away from him?"

She swatted at his firm buttocks, then pulled away. "A virtuous farmer's wife is what they should see at this time of day." So she checked the henhouse for eggs, scrubbed such accumulated laundry as there was and hung it out to dry, and even took the bit of worn carpet from beside the bed outdoors to beat the dust from it. By dusk, when they had eaten soup of her making and the last of the rye bread toasted with cheese, they were so ready for the best part of this game-that-was-no-game that Arkady lost two more buttons from his shirt, and the gathered yoke of Yelena's blouse would need considerable repair.

"Surely a new bride would be submissive to her lord and master," Arkady teased as they fell together onto the bed.

"Of course." Yelena rolled onto her back. "And besides, it's your turn to be on top. So I can use my hands." Which she did, running her fingers over every delicious part of him she could reach, probing between their bodies to find the most rewarding bits and discovering which sorts of touch, and where, could drive his gasps and moans to the highest pitch. When finally he pounded into her with fierce intensity and she raised her hips upward to meet his thrusts, there was no up or down, top or bottom, only shared need mounting higher and higher until it soared past all thought into release.

The drone of planes overhead seemed at first an extension of their heavy breathing. When the pounding of Yelena's heart subsided, she realized suddenly what she was hearing. "Listen!" she said against Arkady's sweaty neck, and raised her head. "They are flying in force to raid the German lines. So many close together! Usually we go in, two or three at a time, at five-minute intervals."

He listened, and after a while rose, went into the main room and opened the window. Yelena joined him with a blanket to wrap around them as they listened to the distant thunder of bombs.

"So many! And look, such fire and smoke!"

"You wish you were with them," Arkady said.

"Of course! Yet I am infinitely grateful that the choice is not mine to make."

They clung together watching until they could stand no longer, then lay entwined in the bed, unable to sleep, though the sound of motorcycles outside the door near dawn startled

Yelena so sharply that she knew she must have been dozing. Arkady was out of bed with his rifle ready before she had tossed aside the blankets.

"Yelena!" Someone pounded at the door. "Yelena, come quickly!" It was Yevgeniya, with a young Russian soldier at her back.

Arkady lowered his gun. Yelena reached him swiftly, again with a blanket to cover their nakedness, and Yevgeniya flashed a broad grin.

"The Germans are falling back!" She could scarcely get the words out fast enough. "We hit the fuel depot at Armavir, and some aircraft as well. Our troops are advancing, only twenty miles away now, and we will meet them halfway."

"Arkady comes too." Yelena disregarded the soldier's gawking and rushed naked into the bedroom to find her clothing.

"Just as well I brought two motorbikes, then," Yevgeniya said cheerfully.

Arkady, as soon as he was dressed, scrawled a note to leave on the table. "My neighbor down the hill brings fresh bread every week, and this is the day. She will see to the care of the sheep and hens."

In seconds, it seemed, they were off, two to a motorcycle. Off to more bombing raids, to the ruined buildings of Stalingrad, to three more years of war; to letters written and sent, and many more days without, and weeks of no news culminating in rushed visits in hospitals. But the day did come at last when Yelena and Arkady climbed the lane to the hillside farm, crossed the threshold and stood together at last where they belonged; and, though no one else was there, both heard far away the achingly sweet music of a balalaika.

SHATTERED

Shanna Germain

While he was gone, I thought about divorcing him. It wouldn't be unheard of. It was happening all over. All my friends whose husbands had gone off to war, they'd found someone on the side. Someone cute and reliable and most important, nearby. Close enough that you could smile at them in the grocery store line. Close enough that they could offer to bag your groceries or take you to dinner. Close enough that you could touch them across a table, across a plate, across the space of the front seat of their car, their fingers and wrists, their hair, the pointy edges of their elbows. Close enough that you could remember the way a collar lies buttoned against a throat, the way it opens under your fingertips like the flap of a letter, holding the promise of joy or grief. Close enough that the morning bed would hold a real body, a physical presence of heat and sleep and *thereness*.

In those days, that alone was enough of a reason for a divorce, because someone wasn't there and someone else was.

I didn't do that. I didn't do the grocery store. Or the dinner.

Or the feel of someone in my bed. Don't think I'm some saint, some holier-than-thou. There was none of that.

The truth of it is that men asked me and I was afraid. The truth is that other men tried to touch me and still I loved him. And as time went on, I became afraid that the only reason I loved my husband so much was because he had not yet come back to me.

Now that he has come back, he goes to meetings. Places with folding chairs and bare lightbulbs, places where the coffee runs free, the cigarette smoke slinks into the fiber of sweaters, the creases of jeans, the kinks of pubic hair.

He talks about the war, and what it meant and what it was like. He sits there in his chair in the back, his palms running over and over on his knees the way he does now. He waits until last to talk. He has to be pushed into it by the dark-haired woman who runs the meetings. In the end, he slurps his coffee, clears his throat, tells this story:

"I wasn't supposed to go ahead of the rest of them. I was supposed to wait outside. But I was impatient and stupid, and there was an explosive...."

Or maybe he doesn't talk at all. I don't know. I don't go to the meetings. I'm not allowed. And he's never talked to me about the war. I make it up in my head, what the horrors were, what the jokes were, how they survived, just enough pieces of them left to glue together and ship back home. What do I know of what he went through?

What I do know is that he comes home to me after the meetings, smelling of fake creamer and words that have been exhaled like stale smoke and of the despair that lingers in the folds of metal chairs.

What I do know is that he comes home and he needs something to do with his fingers. They itch. He chews them sometimes while he watches TV, nibbles roughly on the edges of them as if to eradicate something they remember. Or to remember something they forgot. He likes to open nuts, hard-shelled. Walnuts, mostly. Crack. Crunch. Things breaking into pieces.

Lying in bed, I wait and I wait and I wait. Out in the living room, he breaks his nuts, crackles his knuckles, bites his fingers. I wait some more. Sometimes I fall asleep, but I try not to. I want to be ready for him.

In the early of the morning light, when you think it might be dawn but it's not yet dawn, when it's a new day but there's no light, when the shadows that are just shadows of doors and clothes and lamps morph solid and gain sustenance, I get up and I go to him.

I find my place on his lap and offer myself to him.

In the near dark, he doesn't want to kiss. He wants to bite, to rip and shred. His mouth finds the exposed parts of me and exploits them. Sometimes my neck is bruised so dark it looks like ink splotches decorate my skin. Sometimes my nipples are so purple they turn gray in the bathroom light.

In the near dark, his cold fingers smell of walnuts and the calciumed edges of his teeth. He explores the boundary of my skin—that thin line where I stop being myself and start becoming part of the world—and he interjects himself. I become myself and the world and the him that is this new him. It is not as heavy as I thought it would be, but it is sharp as shrapnel. He licks the hull of me until I'm shiny as steel. He cracks the shell of me with his teeth until I'm nothing, nothing but metal and shine.

Before, he was a quiet man. Even in the bedroom, even in those moments of abandon. A sigh. A groan at most. Our sex wasn't fantastic, but it wasn't awful. Sweet. Vanilla, they call it now.

Vanilla with a swirl of caramel maybe, those occasional, often accidental moments of sweet joy.

I can say that, looking back, as though I know what I'm talking about. As though I *knew* what I was talking about. We were sweet together, and I knew nothing else. He wasn't my first, but he was my longest, and we had a routine, a way of moving together that felt like all there was. Slow kisses and soft caresses and the moment he'd lay me down to enter me. So what if we didn't have butterflies or sparks or if I needed a bit of help with lube? We loved each other and we liked each other and when they sent him away, I lay down in the bed by myself and I masturbated myself to tears.

Now he is not a quiet man. He must make noise, as if to reassure himself that he exists, that the world will not end, that his world will not end, if he gives his position away with a word or a sentence.

When I go to him in these almost-morning hours, he takes my head in his big hands, pushes me down to kneel on the living room carpet.

Now he says: Suck me, cunt.

Now he says: I'm going to finger-fuck you, slut.

He says: I will break you.

I say nothing. I can't anyway, even if I knew what to say. He's got his fingers stuffed in my mouth, his thumb rubbing the edges of my teeth, his fist holding down my tongue.

And even if I could, what would I say?

Now I would say: The push of your hand on the back of my head makes me wet.

Now I would say: I like it when your fingers split me open.

I would say: I want to be broken by you.

No, I wouldn't. I would say *fuck* and *fuck* and the whisper-tug of my fingers in his hair and the slap-sting of my skin beneath his hand and the choked gasp of my breath from my throat.

When I come, he says my name three, five, a hundred times, rapid fire, as though I am a weapon he wields to protect him from the coming day.

Before, he could put me together. I would dissolve under some small and silly thing. A dinner burned. A phone call from my mother. A near accident on the way to the grocery store.

He would walk into whatever room I was in, and he would bend down and wrap his big arms around me and reform me into who I'd been before. Sometimes he would carry me to bed, with his quiet strength, and he would kiss me kiss me kiss me until I cried. And then he would gently fuck me until I cried some more.

Catharsis, I said.

Now he can break me apart. A word. A bite. Two fingers fucking me in one hole, two more in another hole, his tongue in a third. He splits me as easily as if he holds a knife, bone and marrow and skin and pleasure and pain.

He sucks my center from me, triggers every muscle and nerve and pleasure center until I explode into a thousand pieces, a thousand pieces when I thought I only had one. And every piece of every edge comes alive with pleasure, a hundred tiny flares in a place of darkness.

Before the war, he was a man of cock. I don't mean to make him sound callous; he was anything but. There was just no other way. You kissed some, you touched a little, you fucked until he came. Sex by definition.

Don't get me wrong, I liked his cock. Curved up just a little, always darker pink at the end. The way it hardened so quickly in his pants while we kissed. Or against my hand when I touched it. Or, occasionally, rarely, in my mouth.

I liked the way it felt inside me, like he was filling me with something that was only his to give. The best, most personal kind of gift.

Now he is a man of mouth and fingers. Of teeth and tongue and words. We don't talk about his cock now. We don't talk about the mornings, when I help him into his chair. We don't talk about the evenings, when I help him from it and sometimes he cries.

We don't talk about sex as it used to be.

Now sex is predawn light in the living room, me naked and standing before him while he shoves his fingers inside me, a little hard, a little quick, and the pain of it makes my head go fuzzy. The pleasure of it makes me groan and quiver. He holds me aloft with two fingers.

Now sex is when he bends me over his knees, the arm of his chair digging into my stomach. I wriggle like a child, waiting for the sting of that first slap. For the pinch and dig of his nails over my back and ass. Sometimes, if my mouth is free, I beg. *More. Harder. Again.*

When he came back, I thought about divorcing him. It wouldn't be unheard of. It was happening all over. My friends who divorced and remarried, and divorced and married again, they give me looks of pity in the grocery store line. They reach across my plate at dinner or across the car seat and they ask how I am, if I'm okay.

They don't ask why I stay, why I stay, why I stay.

Sometimes I stand before him in his chair, his fingers up inside me as many ways as they'll go, his mouth on my clit, sucking so loudly my face flares hot, and I remember what it was like before.

Sometimes I kneel at his feet, my face pushed into his lap, lapping at his cock that doesn't get hard, getting myself off with my own fingers, and I remember what he was like before.

Sometimes when he's pinching my nipples, nearly breaking the skin of my neck with the sharp suck of his mouth, saying, "You like this, don't you? You little pain whore," I remember what it was like before.

Before the war. When he could fuck me. When he could walk. When he was sweet and vanilla and his touch was softer than ribbons. When I cried myself to sleep thinking, "Is this it? Is this everything?"

And if I could talk at this moment, I would say: this, this moment of pleasure and pain and him saying, "You're mine, slut," and me moaning in pleasure that has no words, this is why I stay. This bruise on my shoulder blade that I touch a hundred times a day just to feel the sparks of desire that light up through my body, this is why I stay. That time of the almost-morning when I crawl on my knees to him as he sits in his chair in the living room, waiting, and that smile, oh god that smile, that tells me I'm in for a world of hurt, that is why I stay.

The truth of it is that he breaks me open and I love every fucked-up bit of it. The truth is that he is broken and I love every shattered piece of him. And I know, I know, that the only reason I love my husband so much is because he never did come back to me.

THE GRUNT
AND THE
DITTY BOP

Craig J. Sorensen

The last workday of trick two's swing shift cycle was done. In her seat on the luxurious tour bus, Jocelyn tugged the hem of her army Class A uniform skirt past the opaque rim of a dark stocking. The bus passed the front gate of Field Station Augsburg, a windowless National Security Agency facility. The massive circular array of antennae called the Elephant Cage loomed off to their left side. After a short but comfortable ride she would be at her barracks room on Sheridan Kaserne.

Jocelyn thrived on the eight-day workweeks known as tricks: six days on, two days off; first a week of days, then swings, then mids, then back to days. This particular two-day hiatus held a rare treat—a day-beggar weekend: Saturday and Sunday off. If it was in the cards, Jocelyn would spend that weekend at Trick π with a guest to be named later.

Trick π was a small apartment that Jocelyn shared with three other women, one each from tricks one through four, who kept the twenty-four-hour vigil at the field station. For

Jocelyn, it was a respite from the endless dots and dashes that escaped from behind the Iron Curtain into her headphones each working shift.

In the bedroom at Trick π was a large wardrobe, fully laden with towels, sheets, blankets and robes, both men's and women's. Across the room from the wardrobe was a dressing table with a polished mirror trained to frame the large, well-used bed. The little round-shouldered fridge in the kitchen was stocked with food, wine, beer and Apfelkorn. In the austere living room was a gaudy chaise lounge that faced a boom box perched on a trunk that was turned on its side. It wasn't much, but Trick π was her escape.

Of course, there was only one way to ensure that the engine repair was an unqualified success: take her out for a spin. It was oh-dark-thirty, and Alexander didn't know which of the four tricks was on days now at the field station. It didn't matter anyway. He did know that their nine-to-five workers would be sleeping on Sheridan Kaserne instead of running in formation like real soldiers.

He took his position in the turret, put on his helmet and gave the order. The engine revved and the ring of tank treads cut through the headphones. As he passed each barracks, there was satisfaction, not only that the mechanic's repair of the M60A3 was a success, but that faces that appeared at windows with bleary eyes were so put out by the intrusion.

One even flipped him the bird.

"You're in the army now," Alex said with a warm salute.

Jocelyn stripped her uniform skirt, jacket and blouse in a smooth motion. She adjusted the black silk panties, corset and garter belt, then hung her dog tags on the gray army bedpost.

She replaced them with a black choker and cameo. She thought to change to white lingerie, so much more striking on her deep bronze skin, but time was wasting. She put on a bright red skirt and jacket but wore no blouse, so the corset would come into view when she bent just so. She pulled the pin from her hair and the tight bun exploded like a hand grenade. Long, wavy chestnut locks fell to her slender waist. She brushed and snags popped loudly.

In the latrine, Jocelyn flossed and polished her pearly teeth. She squeezed a couple of drops of Murine in each eye to camouflage her customary state of exhaustion.

"You look rarin' and ready to go, Sarge. Going to Our Place?" A young woman new to the field station applied burgundy lipstick. Our Place was a bar not far off post, sort of like an English pub crossed with a gasthaus, that was popular among field station soldiers. Usually, it was a laid back place to play backgammon or cribbage and just hang out and listen to tunes.

"Call me Jocelyn. I'm going Top 5 tonight. You ever been?"

"I can't, I'm only a private."

"You can come as my guest. A better ratio of men than Our Place, and a fox like you would be good bait." Jocelyn bobbed her eyebrows, only half-joking.

The private grinned. "If you're looking for men, why not go to the Bonanza?"

Jocelyn rouged her cheeks. "I'm horny, not desperate. Only grunts go to the Bonanza."

Alex adjusted the angle of his light gray button-down shirt so that it lined up perfectly with the zipper of his black slacks and the edge of his belt buckle; even out of uniform, his gig line was razor straight.

Tomorrow, maybe Munich, maybe Ulm or just a local volksmarch. But first, well, a man had needs. His were particularly strong tonight; it had been weeks.

"Night on the town, Sergeant?"

Alex nodded at the young soldier's reflection in the latrine mirror. "Something like that, Private. You?"

"Yes, Sergeant. Are you going to the Bonanza?"

"No." Normally, the answer would be yes. First night of a three-day pass, camaraderie with his crew, half liters of Hasen-Brau and maybe mix it up with some artillery redleg.

Fucking gun bunnies.

Many of the men in his unit turned to the so-called "B girls" at the Bonanza, wallets fat with deutschmarks. But Alex preferred to keep his personal needs to himself. He pressed his left pants pocket to confirm the fresh ribbon of three slender pouches.

Alex set out to a downtown destination, further from post. Some called it Pig Alley. He preferred Forty Mark Park.

When he arrived, it seemed he'd picked a good night. She was quite attractive, less posed, long blond hair, less hardness in her blue eyes, even a fetching, shy smile. Tall and curvy, full breasts and welcoming hips. His kind of woman.

She removed her panties and opened across the bed. As always, he fanned the agreed-upon denomination prominently over the folding chair beside the bed and poised on outspread arms. Her practiced hand reached between them as he groped for the ribbon of foil pouches and held it. He waited for her touch to bring the predictable rise.

Closing time was rapidly approaching at the Top 5 when Jocelyn arrived and found a vacant seat at the bar. She resolved not to let impatience breed poor judgment. There was nothing worse than pretending that those "Meals, Ready to Eat"—grub from bags

that they had served at bivouac back in basic training—were
tasty just because she was hungry.

Same deal with men.

"You with someone?" A deep, gruff voice over her
shoulder.

She turned and tilted her head back. Big, big fellow, blond
hair, piercing Caribbean-blue eyes, handsome, in a grunt sort of
way. Not her usual taste, but no MRE either. "No." Flashed her
seductive smile.

"You do know this is the Top 5 club. As in top five enlisted
grades. Sergeant to sergeant major?" He said it like she didn't
even know rank.

"Is that so?" Her smile fell hard.

"So maybe you should be over at the EM club?" The club for
the lowest four ranks.

"Not that it's any of your business, but..." She pulled her
wallet from her purse and opened it.

Alex studied it like a bartender suspecting a false ID. *SSG
Jocelyn V. D'Ameron.*

Staff sergeant, same as him. He could only assume she was
eighteen since she had military ID; she certainly didn't look that
old. Hell, they practically gave promotions away like Cracker
Jack prizes over at the field station.

She smiled again. "How about you? You allowed in Top 5?"

"Get serious, Sarge."

"So I have to take your word for it, Private?"

He pursed his lips and flipped his wallet open like an under-
cover cop on TV. "Satisfied?"

Jocelyn took the ID. Her eyes shifted between the picture ID
and his face. "Yup, that's you. Triple A."

"Pardon?"

"Alexander A. Archer. Triple A, like the auto club."

"Oh, you're a clever little thing." He drained a full half liter of beer, wiped his chin. "You work at the field station, right?"

"Yeah."

"Bet you work tricks."

"That's a safe bet."

"How much you charge?"

"Don't give it a second thought, Sarge, you couldn't afford it."

"As if I wanted to." He ordered another beer.

"You brought it up."

"It was a joke." Alex never came to Top 5 looking for women. Though the army had recently been fully integrated, he didn't approve. Yes, in World War II it made sense to allow women; but now there were plenty of men who could take the jobs women did.

No, tonight Alex had come to drink away his frustration. His cock hung like a wind sock in the eye of a hurricane, expecting. He turned away and observed as several fellows talked up the small female sergeant and each walked away disappointed.

Yes, Jocelyn was attractive, so when their eyes met again, Alex blurted, "What's your MOS?" He winced. It sounded too much like "what's your sign," and he wasn't interested anyway. His eyes traced along her lapel when it opened as she bent. He returned to her eyes.

"05H."

"Morse intercept, right?"

"Yep. Ditty bop. What unit you from?"

"Third and sixty-third."

"So, you're, like, a tank commander?"

"A lot like one."

She smiled. "Hard work."

"Harder'n listening to a radio all day."

"Try it sometime, buddy. And I'm not talking about listening to AFN."

He liked her less and less. Maybe it would work like that. Seemed the eye of the hurricane was moving off. Wind picking up steadily, but he worried about what hadn't happened at Forty Mark Park.

"Buy you a drink, Triple A?" Her warm knee touched his. He really didn't like that she offered to buy his drink. He hated that he accepted, but accept he did. Then again. And another...

The air smelled of German spring and a nearby bakery. Faded perfume? A hand rubbed his chest. Hard nipples poked his bare back, a soft, sweet sigh in his ear. "I'm still hungry, Triple A." Cool fingers slid down his taut stomach. He hadn't awoken to a woman's touch in ages.

He vaguely recollected a ride off post in a nice VW Golf.

He opened one eye. On the nightstand were two foil pouches torn open, spent rubbers on the top of a nearby garbage can. A slim arm reached for the one unexpended pouch.

"Oh!" He jumped up. "Um, gotta get back on post. I'm— yeah, I'm AWOL." He threw on his scattered clothes haphazardly.

"Thought you said you had—"

"Gotta go, but thanks for..." Coyote ugly, some call it, when a man finds last night's dream girl turned into a morning nightmare. The opposite was true here. He'd remembered her being attractive, but the shapely, compact nude woman who stood on the bed as he headed for the door was startling. Dark skin, dark eyes, luxurious hair. She leapt into his path like an Airborne Ranger.

"Excuse me, uh, Jessica." He slipped by her, butt first.

"It's Jocelyn. Give me a sec to dress, I'll give you a ride back."
She pulled jeans over her naked hips.

"I'm good, Jocelyn."

"But if you're AWOL—" A tight T-shirt squeezed bare
breasts, hard nipples pointed at him.

"I'll be fine." He cupped his hands over his bulging zipper as
he departed and hoped he could find the way back to Sheridan.

Though Jocelyn had sex with him twice, they'd gone so fast.
She worked her clit deftly in the tub, pressed the little sprayer
tight to her pussy and finessed a nice orgasm. She still needed
to feel a man. It was Saturday, and tonight the Top 5 would be
hopping.

Indeed, a half dozen men approached. Jocelyn picked over
them, including one agile fellow who had accompanied her to
Trick π a few months before and with whom she'd had toe-
clenching sex. She instantly regretted sending him away, but did
not take corrective action.

She sat on the same bar stool she'd taken the prior night,
wondering where the night had gone.

"Jocelyn?"

She felt a strange sense of relief. "Didn't get thrown into the
stockade?"

"I was lying. I'm on a three-day pass. I'm a shit liar." Alex
shrugged. "The truth is, I'm just not into casual, you know,
sex."

Jocelyn blurted a laugh then bit her lip. "Really? I mean, you
were pretty Johnny on the spot with the Trojans."

"Well, that was...that's different." He turned away.

"I meant no offense." Actually, she did; his reaction surprised
her.

Big strong grunt, tank commander, his voice kind of choked

up. "I mean, I—look I, I just, I don't like casual, you know, sex."

"Enough said. I'm not your type."

"Really, it's not that. May I?" He pointed to the bar stool by her.

She nodded. And within seconds, the conversation was strangely warm. She didn't quite get him, and she liked this. For the second night of her day-beggar weekend, she did not drive back to the apartment alone.

Alex had never known a woman like her. She was like something from the pages of *Playboy* magazine. Better, really. She was funny, beautiful, dressed so sexy, so at ease with herself. They talked long into the night on a gaudy chaise lounge. She led him to the bed he'd awoken in and squeezed the rubber that he had left behind over his cock.

Jocelyn's face was so beautiful, looking up at him. "Mmm. You feel so good in me, Alex."

A tingle shot up his shaft, his balls tight as a peach. Yes, he had become better at getting down to business where a woman's recompense was a wad of marks. No expectations, no remorse, fast relief, so he focused away from the gorgeous face, body and voice beneath him. He managed to stretch it out until Jocelyn's head turned from side to side and her hips thrust like a jackhammer. She pounded the bed, punctuated by an orgasmic shout. He quickened his pace and drew a deep breath as he careened toward release.

The rubber tore. "Oh shit!" He quickly pulled out. "Do you have another?"

"I can go you one better." Jocelyn bent over his lap. He'd only had this done a couple times and didn't like it. The sensation was strange; it never made him come.

Her tongue swirled around his tip. Like a hair-trigger rifle, he exploded. Jocelyn spat the juice onto his muscular stomach and wiped her chin. "Christ! Why didn't you warn me?"

"I—I'm sorry!"

"At least warn a girl. Shit!"

Not her type of man, Alex. Military bearing, dress-right-dress, muscle-bound Alex. Acted kind of dumb, but he got her strange sense of humor, Alex. And yet, he had left her so satisfied. The memory of his surprise ejaculation even turned her on.

Jocelyn always wore sexy lingerie to work, a secret beneath her uniforms, and though she knew Alex would never approve of this, she felt a similar secret inside him. There was such unrealized potential in him.

She hated that she invited him next Sunday, the next day she'd be at Trick π. He hadn't answered. Now she worried he would not come.

The next Saturday, Alex was as horny as he had ever been. He dressed to go to Forty Mark Park. His hand was on the door of his old Audi, pocket of rolled-up marks. He went back in. He took a deep breath and vowed not to go to Trick π the next day despite Jocelyn's warm invitation but all he could think of was the small apartment just a couple of clicks off post and that damned fascinating, amazing woman.

Jocelyn stripped off her robe. Nothing underneath but silver jewelry. "Undress, please, Alex. Have a seat."

He took the chair by the bed. His jaw slackened as she caressed herself, warmed her nipples with her lips and tongue, then cooled them in a stream of breath. She lay down and demonstrated just how much force her body could take. Pulled her nipples, assaulted her clit, even swatted her ass.

Alex's cock curled toward the ceiling; a glossy line of juice trickled to his hard balls. His hands clenched the arm of the chair like an aviophobe in profound turbulence. Jocelyn thought he might break the arms of the chair. Oh, the power in those hands, those arms, she wanted that power. "Fuck me, Alex!" He'd said he didn't like when she talked dirty, but he was on her like a starving leopard on an ibex. He barely managed to get a rubber on, then reached between them and worked her clit hard. He pounded into her, slapped her ass, confirmed she liked it, and when she nodded, spanked her harder.

He obliged, in all ways. Her legs opened and closed like scissors at his pressure and his audible thrusts. He sucked her nipples hard, then blew on them without missing a stroke, and her orgasm exploded like a supernova. She felt it in every extremity, even her hair. She ascended to the next orgasm almost instantly. Then another. "Oh, fuck. Fuck!"

Her throat was hoarse, and she was coated with their combined sweat when Alex finally let go. She held tight to him. Felt so good, the steadying pace of his heart.

She wanted, needed to know more about him. This need felt strange.

Jocelyn pulled Alex from his clothes as soon as he arrived for their next tryst. He stood like a statue being carved. She gave him a tiptoed kiss, then eased his back to the bed. He opened his arms.

She sat on the side chair, still in a satin bra and panties. "Show me."

"Show you what?"

"How you like it."

"You know how I like it."

"There's always room to learn. You've seen how I like it, and I must say that the result was impressive."

"You do great. Let's do it like that night."

She walked over, kissed him, took his hand and curled his fingers to his cock. "Show me, handsome."

He took a few strokes then stopped. "Let's just...you know."

She urged him two more times, then gave in, but it was as if they had never fucked before, and not in that good "new discovery" way. He was detached, thrust hard, but without passion, no attention to her intensely sensitive breasts, no swats of her ass. She faked an orgasm, he came quickly, and they lay in two awkward heaps.

"Alex, I just wanted to understand more of what you like."

"What's to understand?"

"I mean, like, I showed you. After that you—"

"Look, I don't like to..." He shrugged.

"Show off? I've seen you watch us fuck in the mirror."

He shrugged again.

"You don't like to jerk off? What, you think it's not macho?"

"No, I mean—"

"You think it's better to go to whores?" Adept at interpreting, she figured that much out, but his expression let her know she shouldn't have said it. She covered her mouth.

"Who said I—I—" He jumped up. His pants were on, the rest of his clothes in hand when he went out the front door from Trick π.

"Alex!" She tried to follow, but big as he was, Alex could move fast.

Jocelyn spent the ensuing days off at Our Place, playing backgammon and cribbage. She stopped frequently at the Top 5 and got proposals there, but they weren't tempting. Twice she braved

the Bonanza and fended off eager grunts. Her days off at Trick
π were spent listening to music and sleeping alone on the chaise.
She was strangely relieved each time she headed back to Sheridan to resume barracks life and her next six-day workweek.

She even stopped at Alex's company on Sheridan Kaserne,
but predictably, the orderly room clerk deflected her queries
about Alexander A. Archer.

Jocelyn folded her arms tight after the waitress seated her across
from Alex in the dining room at the Top 5 club. She'd wanted
to grab him a half dozen times, but she was still too mad. She
even pouted, but having never done it before, wasn't sure she
did it right.

"I never saw much point to women in the army, Jocelyn.
Figured there was nothing they could do that was that
special."

"This is how you apologize for leaving me hanging for over
a month?"

"You're a ditty bop. You're supposed to be good at listening,"
Alex said.

She almost laughed. "I'm used to listening to Morse code."

Alex recited the words *dot* and *dash* to form the letters *l-i-
s-t-e-n.*

Jocelyn hid her surprise that he knew Morse. She sat back
and waved for him to continue.

"Jocelyn, I never saw much point to all the attention the
army lavishes on you people. What do you do, listen to a radio?
What's the big deal?"

Silence.

"So tell me where you went for the last month, Alex."

"I've been on leave. It took that long to understand."

"Understand?"

"How tough your job is, or might be. I mean, I can't really know. I don't have your clearance, never been trained in what you do, but I can kind of guess."

"What are you talking about, Alex? Stop being so cryptic."

"I took a month off, learned Morse code, then locked myself away in a hotel room with a shortwave radio. I dialed in wavelengths and copied down what I heard. First, I worked six swings, then two days off, six mids, and two days off. Back to days. Working tricks and listening to blips made me batty, Jocelyn. I fucking barely got through it."

"You really did that? For me?"

"I still think the army mollycoddles you field station bait and ought to make you ride in back of deuce-and-a-halfs or cattle trucks instead of German tour buses, but I do respect what you do." He smiled. "So, can I recharge your battery? Change your tire?"

Jocelyn lifted her brow.

"You know, like the auto club." He held out his hand.

She blurted a laugh and took his hand. "Let me recharge you."

"No, this one is for you."

Alex led her to the chair next to the bed and eased her down. "Jocelyn, I've had a few bad experiences with casual sex along the way. Hurt a really nice girl and—well, yeah, I went to prostitutes. They get to put food on the table, I get my rocks off. And yes, jerking off is for sissies."

Jocelyn laughed, then grabbed her mouth.

"It's worth a good laugh. You messed up my perfect system, and suddenly, it was hard to be without you. So I went off to prove some stupid point that I could do the job you do. The more I realized I couldn't, the more I thought of you. I could only think of you, I'd...I'd fallen in..." He began to undress. "Fallen in love enough to do something I've believed was wrong all my life."

She reached for the top button of her olive drab fatigue top.

He took her hand. "No, just watch."

She hadn't masturbated since he left. Watching took an immense toll on her libido. This was only amplified by the fact that Alex's thick, powerful body looked so beautiful.

Her hands gripped the arms of the chair as he spread his thick legs. He looked so vulnerable, so powerful. His face blossomed with embarrassment. He gripped his cock and demonstrated a twirling motion. He bent the thing downward and this made him gasp. With his other hand, he worked his balls with surprising force. Many of the things he did would never have ever occurred to Jocelyn to do.

As bad as she wanted to slip her fingers down the front of her fatigue pants and plain army panties, she remained fixed to the chair, and she watched how he now went from the rough treatment of his cock to gentle caresses. He stopped.

He took a deep breath, stroked his cock again and let his other hand descend. He pressed one large finger to his anus. He pushed it in and stroked his cock fast. It erupted hard, shooting long tendrils that looked to be in slow motion up his narrow, muscular stomach, over his thick pectoral muscles. Some even reached his chin. He went limp, and she rushed to him. She licked every ounce of the semen from his body. Tasted strangely nice.

She whispered in his ear, "Looks like you ruined my system too."

Four women at a time would take adjacent two-day shifts at the apartment they called Trick π. Adventurous women. Those who were their guests were often surprised at what they found.

Strong women who knew themselves and took control of their sexuality, and sometimes the sexuality of others.

This was in the late seventies, and the residents rode the social changes like surfers. When one of the four members left, usually because she was getting out of the army or rotating to another duty station, another from her trick was recruited to take her place. Not just any woman took a position among the elite of Trick π.

Jocelyn Valentine D'Ameron still had another year in her tour at Field Station Augsburg when she happily surrendered her front door key to an eager replacement. Jocelyn had a new, permanent roommate, and they took a new place in off-post military housing, as was typical for a married couple in the army. They bought a big, brand-new bed, and its headboard pounded the wall like a carpenter driving nails, sometimes days, sometimes swings, sometimes mids. Basically, whenever their very different shifts coincided or conjoined.

Sometimes they took refreshers, and one watched the other pleasure themselves.

Alexander Anderson Archer didn't like that Jocelyn kept her last name. At least, not at first. See, Alex was still an old-world man who had much to learn about modern women.

Jocelyn was just the woman to teach him.

Fortunately, she had found room to learn too.

FIGHTING FOR FRESNO

Ericka Hiatt

O so kicks the door open and carries Arly over the threshold, slung over his shoulder.

She pounds on his back, kicking her legs and yelling, "No, no, no!" at the top of her lungs, laughing so hard she can barely breathe.

He's laughing, too. "Shh, baby, you're gonna get me arrested," he says, but he loves it. He soaks up the joy and the passion she radiates.

The hotel room has an antiseptic smell and it's hot. He kicks the door shut behind them, walks over to the air-conditioning unit and turns it on, balancing her on his left shoulder.

Outside their window, across the parking lot, the motel sign flickers jarringly, FRESNO INN, garish orange and red, lurid green and turquoise. He reaches out to snap the curtains shut.

Arly says, "I'm too heavy, honey, put me down. You're gonna hurt your back."

Oso reaches over with his right hand and slaps her ass, then strokes it, his hand reaching up under her miniskirt. She's soft and round and he grabs a handful of her sweet ass and squeezes. She struggles, laughing still but she makes a sound, it comes from deep in her throat. His heart thumps.

He holds her tighter against his shoulder. "Baby, it's my job to carry the big ol' gun when we patrol. That big ol' gun weighs about fifty pounds more than you do. I hike all day with that goddamn thing weighing me down. Ask me which weight I'd rather schlep around, okay?"

He slings her around into his arms like a sack of potatoes, showing off a bit, grinning like an idiot when she shrieks and grabs his neck, her eyes wide.

Her body lies warm and pliant in his arms as he carries her. He tightens his hold on her, just to feel her softness mold around his fingers. He likes the contrast between the muscles in his arms and her lush body, the soft brown skin of her cleavage, the silky press of her thighs. He lowers his head and kisses between her breasts, nuzzling into them while she squeals and laughs and tries to wriggle free. He catches the lace of her bra in his teeth and pulls it away from her left breast, shaking his head back and forth like a wolf, growling, breathing in her perfume.

Her laughter fades. "Shit..." she whispers, and he raises his head to look into her eyes. She returns his look, wide-eyed, and licks her lips as her eyes flick down to his mouth.

"Please," she says, like it's going to save her life, "please kiss me."

Denny's at nine P.M., the dinner rush. He used to bus tables and it was hard not to think like that. Nine P.M. Dinner rush.

There was still light in the sky away to the west; golden orange and red, deepening to purple as he looked east.

Across from him, she smiled ruefully. "Arlaina Maria Consuela Saez," she admitted.

"Wow, that's beautiful," he said, and meant it.

"It's way too long." She took a too-big drink of her iced tea and gestured at him, swallowing hard. "Your turn, army boy."

She loved to challenge, not the kind that poked around for weakness. When Arly challenged, she did it with laughter, wanting you to challenge her back.

He grinned. "Esteban Roberto De La Rosa."

"How come everybody calls you Oso?"

It wasn't a blind date, though it felt like one. His uncle had said something about running into that nice girl at the supermercado the other day, you know, what was her name, the one who had lived over by the high school, and why didn't Oso give her a call?

He had. He'd asked her out to a movie and dinner at Denny's, nobody's idea of original or romantic, but he only had a few more days' leave and she'd said yes.

And now he watched the way she flung her hands about when she talked, the way her face and her body got into the conversation. She was the most alive person he'd ever met.

"It's *bear* in Spanish." He smiled down at his hands, embarrassed. "I was the biggest of the cousins. My uncle Jorge started calling me Oso when I got to be fourteen and taller than him."

She burst out laughing, then covered her mouth, her eyes wide, when the laugh echoed around the restaurant. He leaned his chin onto one hand and watched her, entranced.

She had long, dark brown hair that swung at her waist and smooth mocha skin that smelled like warm vanilla—the scent reached across the table and teased him every so often. She was built on the plump side. Her breasts strained against her bra, her ass was round and sweet, her waist curved in. He couldn't stop looking into her eyes because of the way they lit up when she looked at him. It made his insides warm.

Two tables away a baby started crying, and his heart leapt up into his throat, every muscle in his body tensing up.

The smell of darkness, dirt, smoke, charred wood and metal and flesh, the crack of rifles, the stench of diesel exhaust, the nasty metallic aftertaste that blood left in the air.

People wailing. A baby screaming, hurt...

Gentle fingers rested on his arm, and he jerked back into the here and now.

She stroked the skin of his forearm, her face calm and soft, giving him an anchor though she couldn't know that. "You been through some shit, haven't you? I wish I could understand," she said.

He swallowed, blinking to clear his eyes, trying to focus on her. "Arly, there's nobody I hate that much, I'd want them to understand what I been through," and then after a moment, "I'm okay, really."

The waitress came to take their order.

He holds her, still cradled in his arms, teases her, brushing her lips with his, flicking his tongue across them. Abruptly he pulls back, turns his head to kiss between her thighs.

She moans again, moving in his arms, and he kisses higher, licking slowly up the inside of her soft round thighs, until he gets to the edge of her miniskirt. He licks the skin where her thighs meet, nuzzling and pushing at her denim skirt with his nose, until his tongue finds the soft ivory satin of her panties. He inhales the scent of baby powder, clean soap, perfume and the sweetness of her pussy. His heart pounds and the blood rushes in his ears.

"Mmm," he growls, low and gravelly, flicks his tongue across her panties, teasing, trying to push between her pussy lips through the satin.

"Son of a *bitch*," she swears, her voice hoarse, her head falling back.

Oso got a Coke for himself, Arly asked for an iced tea, and they ordered their food and an appetizer sampler platter to share.

"You lived here all your life?" he asked after the appetizer plate came. He winced after he said it. It sounded lame.

"Yup. Central Valley, California, baby. Fresno born and bred. How about you?" She picked up a piece of fried mozzarella and dipped it in the bowl of ranch dressing.

He watched the way her long, ruby red nails sparkled in the light. She held her food delicately in her fingertips, turning her head a bit. He watched the way the light shone in her hair, watched how several dark strands fell down her shoulder to lie against the swell of her breast, where her blouse gapped a bit. Her soft red lips closed around the cheese, curved into a smile as she ate.

His throat went dry. "Yup, me too," he answered, and then, "Sorry, I suck at talking to people. I can never think of what to say."

She looked up at him, her eyes warm. "I never know when to shut up. I envy you...."

Another pause.

She said in a rush, "I don't fit too well, most places. I'm too loud, too enthusiastic about everything. I'm too plump to be graceful, too short." She concentrated on picking a chicken strip and wouldn't look at him. "Honestly, I'm too much of everything for most guys.... I was kinda surprised when you called."

"You probably won't remember," he said, "but we met, sort of, before I joined the army. My cousins invited me to a football game. You came with your sister, or something."

"I do remember," she gave him a shy smile. "She was my friend, not my sister. I don't have family." She bit into her chicken strip, ate it, wouldn't look at him. "I remember you," she said again. She looked up at him, quick and embarrassed, and looked away quickly.

The waitress came with their dinner.

He nips at her pussy gently, catches the satin of her panties in his teeth and tugs on them, pulling them aside. He pushes his tongue hard into her, stroking back and forth over her clit and through the soft folds, which isn't easy because her legs are held together by his right arm. He licks again and again, making noises in his throat, raising his right arm, which brings her hips closer to his face. He drives his tongue in and out of her, pressing hard in long strokes. She writhes in his arms, moaning loudly, and he thinks, of course she's going to be a screamer.

The thought of her screaming for him makes his heart pound all over again.

He stops to look up at her. Her eyes are huge in her face, her lips parted. She's panting, he can see how bad she wants him, and he groans as he kisses her hard.

"Make love to me, Oso," she whispers, and he carries her to the bed.

"Yes, ma'am," he answers.

"I never feel safe," Arly said about halfway through her chicken Caesar salad.

"Why not?" Oso asked.

"I have to do everything for myself. I have to go grocery shopping alone and I have to carry all the bags in alone. Every time something breaks, I have to fix it myself. I've been by myself for a really long time."

"I can see how that would be lonely," he said, "but why not safe?"

She searched his face. "When you're out, you know, patrolling or whatever, do you have to watch everything, all the time, by yourself, or do you have other guys to depend on?"

"Oh."

"Yeah," she said, around bites of romaine. "I can't ever just let go. I can't just let someone else handle things." She looked out the window at the headlights, all the late traffic going back and forth. "Sorry. I shouldn't complain. The world is what it is, right? I know things must have been a million times worse for you."

He frowned. "I think that's a reasonable thing to be bugged about. I would be. And bad is bad. You can't measure my real world against yours."

"Oh," was all she said, but her shoulders relaxed, and she turned away from the window to look at him again.

"Jesus, I can't believe how strong you are," she whispers, running her hand up and down his bicep because he's been holding her in his arms all this time.

He gives her a wicked smile, kisses the side of her neck. He's aware every second of how fragile she is, of what he could do to her if he's not careful. He's killed a man with nothing but his hands, and the part of himself he's worried about, the part that may never come out of the desert, that part tries to push into his moment with Arly.

The dirt and the heat and the smoke, the feel of the man's neck bones crunching under his big hands, the weird gurgling sounds and the way the light went out in the man's face....

Oso presses his face into the side of her neck; her skin is clean and sweet, and he inhales her perfume like medicine.

She says something gentle he can't quite hear and holds his face in her hands, pressing little kisses against his forehead and his cheek.

He lays her down onto the bed and stands over her, while she pushes herself back on her elbows and smiles up at him, her eyes half-lidded, her hair falling around her shoulders, her lips gently parted.

She looks vulnerable in that moment, her face and her feelings completely open.

There was a moment when they both went quiet. Voices rose and fell around them, along with the clatter of dishes and the smell of food floating in the air.

Marketplace. Babble of voices. Smell of food. A moment's silence, odd and jarring, then the world turned into light and heat and sound, a shock wave of concussion that blew through him and past him....

He looked toward Arly, as if she were a lifeline, and refused to see anything but her face.

"If I asked you what it was like," she was saying, softly, "would you tell me?"

"No."

Her face closed up.

"It's not that I don't want you to know. It's...." He struggled with the words, said finally, "some asshole blew up a market, and a lot of the pieces went through me. I was lying in dirt that got turned into mud by my own blood, with my body tore up like a piece of meat, and I was one of the lucky ones 'cause I lived.

"Arly," he leaned toward her, "you're perfect, you're like a work of art."

He meant every word. He reached out for her hand, turned it

palm down and spread her fingers under the table lamp. "I was watching your hands—they're beautiful under the light. Your body, your smile, your laugh.... You're like a jewel, baby."

He looked up into her eyes and was surprised to see them sparkle, amazed that he could have such an effect on her. A tear welled up in her eye, spilled onto her cheek.

He swallowed.

"All the horrible shit that's inside me, that I brought back...I don't want that gettin' on to you." He let go of her hand, leaned back, looked out the window.

He kneels on the bed beside her and begins to unbutton her blouse reverently, like she's a gift he's unwrapping. When he gets to her panties, he spreads his hand across her mons as she lies back. His rough fingers catch on the soft satin. He leans to kiss her.

She lifts her hips and he pulls her panties off. He trails kisses down her belly, kissing the place where her pussy lips come together, breathing deep because she smells so good.

She props herself up on her elbows as he stands and looks down at her.

"God damn, baby," he whispers, and all the breath leaves his body, "you are the most beautiful thing I have ever seen...."

"I'm too fat," she says, joking, but he can hear a lifetime of apologies in her voice.

"Arly, love..." he says slowly, "not every guy likes skinny girls." He leans over the bed, catches one of her nipples in his fingers, teases it until it tightens hard.

She closes her eyes and moans.

"My turn now, Oso love," she whispers, sitting back up. "I want to see you...."

He's not a bodybuilder, he likes his steak and eggs and he won't apologize for that, but he has muscle, he's a big man.

Now he strips off his clothes and he tries to stomp down on the things he's afraid of. What if he isn't what she likes? What if she's turned off by the scars?

They start on his left shoulder and spatter across his ribs down to his right hip. They're dark and ugly. He's lucky to be alive, with scars like that, and he wants to tell her that, wants, in a weird way, to be able to be proud of them. But what if she's so turned off she gets up and leaves?

She draws in a breath, sharp and shocked, and he stiffens, hiding his hurt. But then she looks up into his face with soft, sad eyes, whispers, "Oh, baby...." She moves to kneel at the edge of the bed, her hands reaching around his ribs, pulling his body toward her as she softly kisses each scar, from his hipbone up to his shoulder. She is pulling him down onto the bed, murmuring gentle, comforting words into his skin, stroking him all over with her pretty hands, spreading love like a poultice across his hurts.

"The VA was an awful place. It was..." He struggled for an analogy that would do it justice.

The waitress came to refill their coffee cups.

"You know," he said finally, "you know when you go to a big mall on a day right before Christmas?"

She nodded. "Oh yeah. Hell yeah."

"And you're going through the parking lot, only you can't go more than two feet before some asshole is getting in your way, or crossing the street right in front of your car or stealing the only parking space you found in a half hour of looking?"

"Yup," she said again.

"Okay, and then you actually find a parking space and you get inside the mall and every store is packed with bat-shit-crazy people. They're cutting each other off and grabbing things out of each other's hands and pushing and shoving? You're standing

there watching this with your ears ringing from the noise, knowing you're not gonna find anything on your list, and if you do find anything, they're not gonna have it in the size you want, and if they do somehow have it in the size you want, there's no fucking way you're going to get a salesperson to actually ring it up before Christmas is over?"

"This is a seriously fucked-up analogy," she opined.

"Yup," he said. "Welcome to the glory of bureaucracy that is the Veterans Administration."

"So," she said, "the VA is a seriously fucked-up analogy for the real world?"

He had to stop and think about that. "God, I hope not, but from what I've seen of the world, it might be. Afghanistan, anyway. Iraq, maybe. But definitely Afghanistan."

"Honey," she said, suddenly quiet and serious, "I don't know what any of those places are like, but I don't want to believe they're the real world. I really don't."

"Arly, baby," he said quietly, "sometimes my world is Fresno-shaped, but most of the time now it's Afghanistan-shaped. I don't know why I gotta be over there, fighting people who have nothing to do with me, but maybe it's so your world gets to stay Fresno-shaped. Or, anyway, that's what I been told." He leaned his elbows on the table, reached out to tuck a strand of her hair behind her ear. "That would make it okay, I think."

The way she looked back at him, that made him feel twenty feet tall.

He pulls her up to kiss her, his rough, broad hands burying themselves in the heavy silk of her hair. The way she moans into his mouth and leans her body into his chest makes him flush hot. He catches her wrists and pushes her down toward his cock, his heart pounding, hoping she's okay with it, thinking she is....

She spreads her hands across his thighs and teases him with her lips and her tongue. She's growling now, deep in her throat, and she looks up at him, her eyes half-lidded again.

She twists her head back and forth, working her tongue around and over the head of his cock. Her eyes fall closed, her fingertips hold him gently, and he reaches over and turns on the bedside lamp so the light sparkles on her ruby red nails.

He can only stand it for a moment or two more before he has to pull her up or orgasm right then and there. He wants to be inside her now, wants her so bad he can hardly think for the blood pounding through his brain.

She takes his hands and lies back on the bed, her face wreathed in secret smiles, pulling him down on top of her. She strokes down his ribs as he positions himself. She closes her eyes and her head falls back. She hisses as slowly, slowly, he pushes into the soft warmth she offers him, going as deep as he can.

The feeling is so intense he groans and has to pause, his forehead falling to hers. Her hands rise to his face and her lips press against his cheeks. She strokes his hair as she whispers soft, sweet things he only barely hears.

He begins to move in her and they both cry out every time he pushes deep. His whole body tightens.

Her fingers stroking his face, his shoulders, his chest. She whispers love at him: "You're home, baby, come on home...."

Home, he thinks as he makes love to her, as he bends his head to suck on her huge, plump nipples, his cock stroking in and out of her glorious body.

Home.

The waitress came back and asked them if they wanted dessert. Arly looked through the menu.

Oso watched her *ooh* and *aah*, and was charmed.

She held out her arm to him. "Check, will you? I'm not sure what I feel like."

Bemused, it took him a moment to guess her meaning. *Check what I feel like.... What I FEEL like? Oh.*

He squeezed up and down her arm a few times, his big hand wrapping easily around her forearm. "Hmm. Not sure what you feel like. Soft and sweet?" he said finally.

She burst out laughing. "Wow, *you're* no help."

"Allow me," he said in his best gentleman voice.

The waitress stared down at them. He wondered how often she had to stand there and watch idiots fall in love. Probably too often, from the look on her face.

"Triple banana split," he told her, "extra fudge and strawberry sauce, and leave the can of whipped cream."

The woman smiled tiredly. "I'll bring you each a bib."

"And extra cherries," he called after her.

She really did bring two bibs and they really did wear them.

They ate the ice cream, fighting with their spoons like swords over the last bit of banana and chocolate. The entire restaurant stared when Arly shot her arms up in the air, crowing with delight as she captured and downed it before he could wrestle it away from her.

Oso high-fived her. "You play to win."

"No quarter asked or given." She smiled smugly. Then she said, "You thought I was kidding when I said I was too much of everything. Most guys freak when I don't let them win."

There was something sad about that image, Arly being loud and strong and, well...just being Arly, and then he imagined her wilting under some insecure asshole's disapproval.

It made his fists itch.

He leaned toward her. "That's because most guys are weaker than you," he said.

She leaned forward as well; her lips were so close. His palms prickled and his mouth went dry.

She responded the only way she could, being Arly. "And you're not?"

"Nope," he answered, "I'm stronger than you. You can be too much of everything, and it'll just break on me like waves, I'll just want more."

She leaned back, her head cocked to one side.

He drew up his courage then, and said, "Arly, honey...make love to me. Please...."

A slow smile dawned across her face. She laughed and didn't bother to cover her mouth when people stared this time.

"*Hell* yes!"

He threw two twenties onto the table and they were out of there.

Arly gritted her teeth, her eyes squeezing shut. She threw her head back, her hair spreading out like waves of dark silk, as he watched the orgasm sweep over her. She screamed and her fingers bit into his shoulders, her back arching beneath him, her legs wrapping tight around his thighs.

The sight of her losing herself in an agony of pleasure was what pushed him into his. Oso's whole body tightened in a wave that started at his feet and spread through him until it centered on his cock.

He came like thunder. He yelled around his clenched jaw, pushing hard a few more times, then slowing, in and out, in and out, a pause, one last long slow thrust as he groaned.

And then he gathered Arly into his arms and held her as tight as he could while his heart pounded against his ribs and the sweat on his body cooled slowly.

She kept her legs wrapped around his thighs, her arms around his ribs, as if she couldn't stand an inch of space between them. In the dim light of the lamp they'd left on, he could see the pulse jump at her throat. He pushed the dark and matted hair back from her forehead and planted gentle kisses across her skin.

She smiled sleepily and snuggled down into his arms. He reached over to turn off the light and then pulled the blankets up over them. For a while they slept.

"What is the real world?" he whispered against her hair, sometime much later.

"Not Afghanistan," she reminded him. "Or the VA. We pretty much decided that already. Why?"

"Arly, honey, I don't know what the hell I'm doing, going back to some country thousands of miles away to fight for 'Truth, Justice and the American Way' as it applies to Fresno, California. All you gotta see is one dead body, you know, you just got to get shot at a few times, and everything gets dark and fucked up. It's like a taste you can never get out of your mouth; it ruins everything."

Arly drew in a deep breath. He could feel her ribs move and he thought maybe he was holding her too tight. He loosened up a bit, but she only burrowed closer.

After a long silence, she said, "Fight for me, baby. Fight so you can come back to me. Fight because I need to be safe, and right here, right now, lying in your arms, this is the safest I've ever felt in my life. Fight because I need you." She tilted her head back to look up at him. "Fresno can be me, okay? *I'm* Fresno."

"Yeah," he said, blinking away all the ugly stuff, concentrating on the way she smelled and the feel of her body against his. "Okay. Make love to me again, Fresno...."

HOMECOMING

Kelly Maher

The acrid tang of burned milk filled the kitchen as she collapsed to the floor, tears running down her face. Molly laid her head on her knees, no longer able to maintain the façade. Three days ago, her world had imploded with no one the wiser.

She'd understood the possibility, thought she'd prepared for it, but never could have comprehended the utter gutting of self.

A side story in the paper already overwhelmed by the news of virulent politics and ghastly murders. The loss of an entire Marine platoon out on patrol two days before was a blip on the radar. The only reason she'd even caught the story was because of the damn Google Alert she'd set up. Due to her job as a traveling consultant based out of DC, she'd never had the chance to meet and get to know any of the spouses and girlfriends of David's unit. Molly doubted they even knew she existed.

Fresh waves of grief smothered her in suffocating blackness.

Grief for how little time they'd been able to spend together. Grief for the future they'd never have to rectify that loss.

Time slid by in a pitch-black ooze. The distant ringing of her phone barely registered. Even if she had wanted to respond to the summons, her body had turned into a numb lump. A woman who had once prided herself on answering with a smile within two rings now wished the world would disappear into the black hole where her soul had once resided.

She curled up, back pressed against the sharp lower edge of her cabinets. The pain focused her mind for a moment, and she thought of the milk before remembering she'd moved the pan from the hot burner. Tears leaked down onto her arm. She thought of the first time she'd met David.

His smile, slow and serious, melted her heart. They'd run into each other at the embassy open houses. Twice in one night. She'd first spotted him at Australia but had let self-doubt force her into letting the moment slide away. There was no way a man that magnetic would look twice at her. An hour later she'd been reaching for small weisswurst at Germany when she'd been bumped from behind. The deep voice expressing abject apologies sent a bolt of lust through her system. Even before turning to discover who the man was, she was wishing it was him.

It was.

She'd teased him about engineering the bump, and she'd gotten the smile in return. They'd spent that first night walking down Embassy Row to Dupont Circle and dancing until the wee hours of the morning. They'd eventually landed in the apartment she'd been renting at the time. Even now, in her paralyzing agony, her body responded to the remembered pleasure.

The year since had been one of lazy weekends and hurried

hookups. He'd been stationed down in Norfolk, but whenever he'd had leave, he made the trip up as long as she wasn't out of town on an assignment.

A week before he shipped out to Afghanistan, she'd closed on a gorgeous old Victorian in Takoma Park. It gave her the sense of permanence she'd craved as a kid shuffled around from foster home to foster home. She knew she'd gotten through the system with minimal scars, but the shared lack of blood family was a point that had drawn her and David closer. He was close to retiring and expected this to be his last deployment. They'd made, *she'd* made, giddy plans of how they'd remodel the kitchen and build a sunroom off the back. He'd just stood back and said, "Whatever you want, honey."

One week later, instead of kissing him good-bye down in Norfolk as she'd planned, she'd been on her way to Seattle to triage the near-catastrophic meltdown of a project another team had been working on. With all the preparations he needed to do for deployment, they hadn't even managed one last night together.

She'd gotten a bonus and a promotion out of the sacrifice, but if she'd had to do it all over again, she would have quit rather than miss seeing David one last time.

A knock rattled the front door. She scrunched up closer to the cabinet. Every morning since discovering the story, she'd dutifully called in sick to work so they would know she was alive and wouldn't call the police on her for a safety check. This morning her secretary had sounded worried, but Molly couldn't bring herself to fully reassure Diane of her well-being. Instead, she'd let loose that she was dealing with a death in the family. No one at work knew that much about her past, so Diane had let it go at that.

The knocking finally stopped and Molly relaxed a fraction.

She didn't even know who to call to find out about where David was going to be buried. If he could be buried. Had his body been recovered?

Glass from the back door shattered and she screamed.

A dark figure in black came through as the door opened. She couldn't stop screaming. Why weren't her neighbors coming?

She scrambled back to the corner of the cabinets, pulling herself up to reach for the knives in the butcher's block.

"Molly."

Her body froze. Then her knees dissolved and she sank once more to the floor, head shaking. It was a ghost. Wasn't it? But ghosts couldn't break into houses. He went to his knees, meeting her on the floor.

This time her reach was for the chiseled jaw, the skin drawn tight and pale. "You're dead."

Rough calluses caressed her hand as he pressed her palm against his cheek. "No. They tried. I'm here."

"You're dead. Everyone died. They said *everyone* died."

He shook his head. "I'm here, Molly, I'm here."

She clutched her arms around his shoulders and attached herself to him like a barnacle. "You're dead, you're dead, you're dead."

Her litany of disbelief was answered by his of reassurance. She dug her fingers into the hard muscles of his back and shoulders. She wanted to merge him into her so he would never leave her again. A heartbeat's separation would be too much.

He winnowed his hands into her hair and pulled her back into his hold. She tried to fight, but he molded his lips to hers. She sucked on his lower lip, nipped it with her teeth.

Growls emanated from his chest, rumbling through both of them. His tongue speared into her. Claimed her. Thrust and retreat. Possession. Life.

She needed him in her right then. Covering her. Filling her. Uniting them.

Tearing at his shirt, she tried to rip it off him, but couldn't find purchase. He got the message, though, and broke the kiss long enough to pull it off. When his arms were tangled up in the heavy cotton, she took advantage and stroked her hands across taut skin. Took note of large patches of bruises, scrapes, lacerations. Kissed his injuries as she found them.

"Molly."

She tried to shake him off, but he prevailed, sinking his mouth against hers once more. In one motion, she pushed off her leggings and panties. Winding her legs carefully around his waist, she ground against the erection that strained against the fly of his pants. This time he hissed.

She froze in his arms. "Did I hurt you?"

"No. Come back."

She pushed one hand against the brick wall of his chest. "Did. I. Hurt you?"

He cupped her jaw. Massaged. Met her eyes straight on. "No. You could never hurt me. You just reminded me I should probably go a little slower." He breathed out a sigh. "And we should probably head up to the bedroom. Christen it properly. We didn't get a chance before I shipped out."

"David..."

She didn't know what to say. Drank in the sight of his close-cropped dark brown hair, silvering in spots. The laugh lines at the corners of his chocolate eyes. The Roman nose that had been in one too many bar fights when he was younger.

He really is here.

She lifted her mouth to kiss him again, but before she could make contact, he stood and lifted her up into his arms.

"David. You're hurt." She tried to escape his hold, but he

clamped her legs together with one arm and pressed her torso tight to his.

"Don't fight me. You might hurt me more."

She sighed. When David got all autocratic master seargeanty on her, there was no arguing. He rarely pulled out that tone of voice, and when he did it was always for a good reason. She subsided against him and reveled in the sensation of being in his arms once more.

"Did you take the front bedroom like you'd talked about?"

"Yes."

That was it. No more words were needed. For now. She stroked her palm against his chest, happiness bursting through her as she felt the flex and release of muscle as he maneuvered them up the twisting staircase.

She hadn't made the bed since the morning the story broke, and most of the covers had fallen off during the restless hours she'd managed a semblance of sleep.

He laid her down amidst the chaos and stood there.

"My princess."

For the first time since he'd called her that, she didn't snort, only opened her arms—and her legs—to him.

He sank one knee down beside her thigh and placed a kiss at the throb of her pulse in the hollow of her throat. He took hold of the collar of her T-shirt and ripped it down the middle. She struggled out of the rags and wrapped her arms around him. Stroked her hands down his back, cupped his shoulder joints.

Kisses rained down her body as he relearned her with the same studiousness he applied to tactical guidebooks. The rough skin of his fingers scraped down her hips, outside of her thighs, back up again, circling where she craved his attentions. Finally, one finger traced the lips of her sex. Liquid heat greeted him. She spread her legs open even further to encourage him. He tweaked her clit in acknowledgment, but only played on the outer edges.

She groaned. "David, please..."

He nipped at the skin above her belly button. She took the hint. He'd get there in his own time. How he controlled himself when she wanted him pounding into her, reaffirming his vitality, their future... Her thoughts drifted when he covered her with his mouth and sucked on her clit. Hard. Liquid gold coated her nerves. Two fingers speared up into her and coaxed brilliant diamond starbursts to explode. Her body bowed under the firestorm of pleasure. She counted each heartbeat from the moment of climax to when his hard cock replaced his fingers.

This time her tears were for joy. Even now, he took his time. Elicited yet another climax out of her emotionally wrecked body. His eyes locked on hers, refusing to let her retreat as he joined her.

Molly figured she must have blacked out even though she would have sworn her eyes never closed. She didn't want to fall asleep and wake only to find this to be a dream. The heavy weight of his body lifting off her finally broke through her stupor. Her fingers turned into claws as she fought him leaving.

His hands caressed her arms, tried to loosen the locked muscles. "It's okay, baby. I'm not going anywhere. I just have to go lock the door and grab my bag. I'm coming right back. I swear."

She nodded, but still needed his help to release him.

He hitched his pants back up around his waist and fastened the fly before leaving her room. She strained her hearing to track his movements through the house. First the stairs, then the beat of his boots against the hardwood floors of the living and dining rooms. Crinkling as he crossed the glass-strewn tile floor of the kitchen.

She heard the door close and then the sounds repeated in reverse.

Back in her room, he stripped out of boots and pants. Moonlight glimmered on his naked body, and she bit her lip. His injuries were even more extensive than she'd first thought. Two dark lines crisscrossed one thigh. Muscles strained against skin and stitches as he bent to pull something out of his bag. "David..."

He looked over to her and then down to where her gaze was fixated on the black stitches holding him together.

"I'll tell you later." He came back to the bed and lay down next to her. Placed his fist against her heart. "When you had to cancel on the deployment ceremony, I promised myself that I would move heaven and earth to make sure you got this."

"I wanted to be there."

He pressed a quick kiss against her lips. "I know you did, honey. I know you did. In a way, I'm glad you did miss it. I was all the more determined to make it back to you." He undid his fist and she felt the warmth of metal hitting her left breast.

She reached up and took the ring from where it lay.

"You have my heart, Molly. Will you marry me? Be my family?"

She'd thought the joy that had filled her earlier was as much joy as she could contain. She'd been wrong, and she hoped he would prove her wrong more and more every day. She held the ring up to the shaft of moonlight and caught the flare of blood red in the stone.

"It's a ruby."

His fingers stroked up and down her midriff. "Red's the color of blood, blood is life, and you're my life, Mol. I will always, *always* come back to you."

She looked into his eyes and let the truth of his words seep

into her bones. "I love you, David. When I thought you died..."
Her breath hitched, the thought choking her once more.

"Always, Molly, I promise."

She nodded and handed him the ring to slip onto her finger.
She kissed him, this man who risked his life for his country and
survived hell to get back to her.

"Yes."

PASSING OUT PASSION

Lucy Felthouse

As we filed into the mess, I glanced to my left and caught my mother's eye. We shared a smile. From my other side, my dad grabbed my hand and gave it a quick squeeze before letting go. It had been a tough twelve weeks, but now that my younger brother Shane had successfully completed his basic training for the British Army, we were overwhelmed with pride. We'd just watched him and his colleagues at their passing-out parade, complete with the pomp and ceremony Brits are famous for, and were heading indoors for some food, drink and celebrations.

I could hardly wait to see Shane and tell him how proud of him I was, but I knew that the recruits had a few formalities to take care of before they could head into the mess and be with us. Throughout the parade, I'd barely taken my eyes off the spectacle before me. The band and the recruits had mesmerized me with their well-rehearsed routines, and when I'd finally spotted Shane, I'd welled up. My little brother. Though of course, he's not all that little. He's four years younger than me, yet when we stand side by side I barely come up to his shoulder.

Now, though, I looked around at the other families and friends who'd also come to celebrate their loved ones' achievements. There were lots of women hugging and men shaking hands and slapping backs. There were people closer to my age, too, the brothers and sisters of the recruits, and also girlfriends and boyfriends.

"Christina."

My mother's voice tugged me out of my thoughts, and I turned to face her with a smile.

"Come on, dear, your father's gone over there to get us a table."

I looked in the direction she was pointing and spotted him. My mother walked toward the table she'd indicated. The room was filling rapidly and I quickly lost her in the squeeze of bodies.

I slipped between people with a polite smile and the occasional "excuse me" if they hadn't seen me. Then I got to a group of people that were so tightly packed together and laughing raucously that I had to tap one of the group on the shoulder. The guy spun around faster than I'd expected, almost knocking me over in the process. He reached out and grabbed my elbow to steady me, then our eyes met and I gasped before I could stop it. He was obviously just as surprised as I, as his blue eyes widened and his grip on my arm became tighter. My resultant frown made him realize what he was doing, as he let go of me and finally opened his mouth.

"Hey!" His previous shock forgotten, his face transformed from surprised to happy. "What are you doing here?"

My mouth suddenly dry, I gulped a couple of times and forced myself to speak before he thought I was a complete moron.

"We're here for my little brother, Shane. He just passed out."

"*That's* why I recognized the name! My little brother just completed training, too."

He carried on talking, and although I was gazing at his face, I had no idea what he was saying. My mind was desperately trying to process the fact that he was here at all. Phil Ashdown, at my brother's passing-out parade. Granted, it was *his* brother's parade, too, but my brain refused to compute that part. Instead, it went into total meltdown.

"Anyway, Phil, it was lovely talking to you, but I have to go see my parents and Shane. Take care."

He looked surprised at my cutting him off mid-sentence, then recovered quickly and replied, "Sure. Maybe I can catch up with you later?"

I slipped past him without replying and dashed toward the table where my mum and dad were sitting, waiting for me. At the same time, I spotted Shane crossing the room and detoured to give him a hug.

"Shane!"

He picked me up and swung me around as though I weighed nothing, then set me back down. A smile spread across his handsome, good-natured face.

"Hey, sis! I missed you, too!"

We laughed, then I slipped my arm through his and led him toward our table. As our parents stood and greeted Shane, I sat down. I'd deliberately chosen a seat with the wall behind it. I've always hated the idea of someone creeping up behind me, and I adore people-watching, so it was a careful choice. In this case, though, it was one person in particular I wanted to watch.

Phil Ashdown. I could still scarcely believe he was here. Or, come to think about it, that I'd been rude to him and run off. It was totally out of character for me to be rude to anyone, even someone

I didn't like. And I certainly didn't dislike Phil Ashdown.

Quite the opposite, in fact.

I pushed Phil out of my mind and listened as Shane chatted animatedly about the crazy things he'd been put through in his training period. The more I listened, the prouder I was of my brother for completing his training, and I told him so. My parents agreed wholeheartedly, particularly my mother, who gave him another hug and left a generous smudge of cerise lipstick on his cheek.

He waved his hand dismissively, as though it had been nothing but a stroll in the park, but the pink twinge that flushed his cheeks gave him away. I grinned at him, ready to dish out some of the sisterly teasing I hadn't been able to administer for months, when out of the corner of my eye I saw two people approaching our table. I assumed one of them was a colleague of Shane's, given he wore the same dress uniform, and Phil was with him. I shuffled down in my seat, pointlessly hoping that he wouldn't notice me sitting there.

As they drew up to the table, the guy in the uniform tapped Shane on the shoulder. Shane turned, then jumped out of his seat with a grin and gave his colleague a hug. My stomach lurched. This wasn't anywhere good.

"Hey, man! We did it!" The boys clapped each other on the back, then turned to face my parents and me as Shane managed the introductions.

"Everyone, this is my good buddy, Paul Ashdown. Paul, this is my mum, my dad, and my sister, Christina."

Paul gave a wave and a grin, then swept his arm back to indicate Phil standing just behind him.

"Nice to meet you. This is my brother, Phil. He's in the army, too. But he's *much* older than me, so he's practically a veteran."

Paul nudged his brother jovially and got a fierce scowl in response.

I bit my lip to hold back a smirk, and Phil shot me a look. My face immediately straightened, then filled with heat. He continued to stare, but my mother had invited the Ashdown boys to sit with us and no one else was taking any notice of me. Phil took his seat wordlessly, continuing to gaze at me until I was begging any deity or supernatural being that would listen to make the ground open up and swallow me whole.

Unfortunately, I remained exactly where I was. I pointedly ignored Phil and listened to the boys chatting with my parents. However, my peripheral vision told me that I was still being stared at, and it was seriously starting to piss me off. If not for the others, I would have given him a piece of my mind.

Phil obviously had a few things he wanted to say to me, too, as he stood up and said, "Would anybody like a drink? Christina, would you mind helping me?"

I watched a strange look pass between my brother and Paul. My mother's face, already perfectly happy, brightened even further. *Wonderful,* I thought, *they're matchmaking us now. That's all I need.*

I didn't see any way I could get out of it without appearing either rude or bonkers, so I stood up with a tight smile and made my way around the table as Phil took everyone's orders, ignoring the silly eyebrow wriggling and inane grinning my mother was partaking in. Then we headed in the direction of the makeshift bar.

As soon as we were out of earshot of the table, Phil said, "What the hell is wrong with you, Christina? First you don't want to talk to me, and now you're acting like we never met before! I didn't realize you hated me that much."

I glanced across at him and shook my head. *Moron.* How

could he possibly think I hated him? I took in his cropped blond hair, sparkling blue eyes, chiseled jaw and his smokin' hot body, and decided the only people that could possibly hate Phil Ashdown were other guys. After all, with him in the room, most girls wouldn't want to look at anyone else. I certainly didn't.

"I don't hate you, Phil." The words *in fact, I'm still in love with you* were left unsaid, but they floated around my head, threatening to creep out when I least expected it.

"So what's up? Why are you being like this?"

His voice had risen in his irritation and a few people glanced in our direction. I grabbed Phil's arm and steered him outside where we could talk in private.

"Firstly, don't speak to me like that. Secondly, if you must know, I'm being like this because I don't know how *else to be.*"

"I don't understand."

I wasn't surprised. Phil may be hot, but he wasn't always the quickest on the uptake, particularly when it came to matters of the heart.

"Really? You don't understand? Well, let me spell it out for you. We met at university, we dated, I fell for you and thought we had a future. Then you announced that after you graduated you were going to join the army and didn't think it would be fair on me to continue our relationship, effectively ripping my heart out of my chest and stomping on it. Then we end up here together and you expect me to act normal. Get it now?"

Phil looked so stunned and confused that I almost felt sorry for him. Almost.

"But I thought you wanted to break up."

Now it was my turn to be confused.

"What? How could you even think that?"

"You didn't disagree. When I said I thought it would be

too difficult to maintain a long-distance relationship, you just accepted it. I figured it was what *you* wanted."

For once, I kind of understood his logic. I remembered the conversation well and he was right. I'd followed his comment with a shrug and an *okay* and left. What he didn't know was that I'd headed straight back to my dorm room, locked the door and cried into my pillow until I'd fallen asleep, exhausted. In my mind, it hadn't been up for discussion. He was dumping me, and that was that. I'd avoided him for the rest of the term, then we'd graduated and got on with our separate lives.

I repeated this thought process to Phil, and by the time I'd finished his eyebrows were almost in his hair.

"You're kidding." It wasn't a question. "So you're telling me that you didn't want to split up either?"

"What do you mean, either? It was your stupid idea!"

Phil shook his head. "Sounds like we've both been stupid. Listen, Christina, I *never* wanted to break up with you. I knew that when I joined the army it would be tough to maintain a relationship, so I gave you the option to get out. When you took it without hesitation and then ignored me for the rest of the year, I figured I'd been dumped!"

We looked at one another in silence, though I was sure he must be able to hear my heart pounding in my chest. I couldn't get my head around the conversation we were having. All those years ago, neither of us had wanted to break up, and yet we'd done it anyway. Stupid wasn't the word.

I couldn't think of a single thing to say to make things right, and given Phil's continued silence, neither could he. All I knew for sure was that we'd both fucked up royally and that I was still madly in love with him. I dropped my gaze before he saw the tears welling up in my eyes.

He knew, though. He put a hand beneath my chin and lifted

my head. I blinked furiously and willed the tears to stop. Phil and I had had the worst possible misunderstanding all those years ago, and there was nothing we could do about it. It was too late.

Stroking his thumbs across my cheeks to wipe away the years, Phil said, "Please don't cry, C. It was a long time ago."

The use of the nickname only he used for me coupled with his brush-off of the situation just made me more upset. I pulled away from him and covered my face with my hands.

"Wh-what did I say now?"

My sadness and grief had started to morph into anger, and I moved my hands and stared him in the face.

"Oh, it's all very well for you, isn't it?" I repeated his words mockingly, "*It was a long time ago.* Well, that may be true, but unfortunately for me, I still fucking love you!"

I made to storm past him and back into the mess, but he grabbed me around the waist and yanked me back. I yelped and tried to wriggle out of his grasp, but his strong, muscular arms meant I had no hope of escape. I sighed and stopped moving, and my body slowly became aware of the big, firm one pressed against it, not to mention a big firm something else pushing against my bottom.

Despite my anger and upset, my traitorous hormones reacted to the situation and sent a bolt of lust rushing through my body. My nipples hardened and a delicious heat flickered between my thighs. I gulped as I remembered just how skilled Phil was at scratching that particular itch, then renewed my wriggling. I had to get away. There was no way I could let him know I was horny because if he came on to me, I wouldn't be able to resist. He'd always been my weakness. Bastard.

"C, stop it. Just calm down. I'm going to let you go. Will you stay where you are so we can talk?"

I nodded, unwilling to speak for fear I'd say something else that was completely insane. Though after telling him I still loved him, I wasn't sure how much more foolish I could get.

Phil slowly released me, and for a split second, I thought about bolting. That is, until he spoke.

"I still *fucking* love you, too."

I turned to face him, my eyes wide. For what felt like the millionth time that day, a multitude of emotions rushed through me and I struggled to process them all. I just stood there, gaping like a fish. Finally, my brain caught up. Before my rational side knew what was going on, my right hand had delivered a hearty slap to Phil's gorgeous face. My mouth had also started spouting angry nonsense.

"Well, that's all right then, isn't it? The fact we've been apart for all these years for *no fucking reason* means nothing because we still love each other! Could you *be* any more stupid?"

I may have been attacking Phil, but really I was furious with myself, too. We were both to blame.

I opened my mouth again, ready to launch another tirade of abuse, but Phil countered it with a movement of his own. He reached down and cupped my face in his big, warm hands, leaned down so his face was on a level with mine and said, "God, you're sexy when you're angry."

Before I had a chance to react, he kissed me. As his lips touched mine, all the stiffness and tension left my body, followed swiftly by the anger. In fact, had he not chosen that moment to slip his arms around my waist, the weakness in my knees probably would have caused me to fall over.

Pulled tightly to him, I could feel his erection pressing against my abdomen. Lust trickled its way into my knickers, and I opened my mouth to return his kiss. His tongue immediately thrust between my lips and sought out mine. I reached around him and cupped his ass in my hands as our kiss deepened.

It was some time before we pulled apart. When we eventually did, we were both gasping, and I suspected my facial expression mirrored Phil's flushed, lust-addled one. We gazed at one another for a couple of seconds, then a strange movement from Phil made me look down and see what the problem was. A giggle escaped my lips as I watched him try to rearrange his stiff cock beneath his pants.

"What?" he asked, grinning at me. "I can't help it if you make me horny, can I? There was a time when you'd have dragged me to a secluded spot for a little relief."

"And what makes you think I won't do that now?" I gave him what I hoped was my sauciest grin, then looked around for somewhere even more private for us to go.

"Oh, I dunno," he said, clearly thinking I was bluffing, "only the fact that our families and lots of strangers are inside that building."

"True," I replied, nodding. "But they're not inside *that* one."

I pointed to a building at the other side of the courtyard. I had no idea what was inside it, and to be honest, I didn't really care. I walked quickly toward it, hoping that we'd get there before anyone saw us. A glance over my shoulder told me that Phil wasn't far behind.

I tried the door handle, heaving a sigh of relief as it gave beneath my hand. Phil quickly moved behind me and shoved me hurriedly inside, pushing the door shut and locking it. He then held his index finger to his lips, strode across the room and stuck his head around a couple of doorways to make sure we were alone.

He gave a curt nod and said, "Thank fuck for that. Now come here."

Raising an eyebrow, I replied cockily, "Why don't *you* come here?"

Letting out a noise that was somewhere between a sigh and a growl, Phil moved quickly across the room toward me. Putting his hands on my hips, he steered me until my back was pressed against the door. Then he moved in for another kiss. A spine-melting, toe-tingling, hair-standing-on-end kind of a kiss.

We clung together in our passion, Phil's hands tangled in my hair and my fingers gripping handfuls of his white T-shirt. We'd both look a complete state when we headed back to the party, but right at that moment, it was the last thing my mind. Especially when Phil's right hand left my hair and began to stroke its way down my body.

His fingers trailed slowly down the side of my neck, leaving goose bumps in their wake. Reaching my left breast, he cupped it through my dress, then pinched the nipple hard enough to make me twist my face away from his and squeal. My clit began to throb as though it were that particular bundle of nerve endings he'd tweaked. I arched my back, suddenly desperate for him to touch me between my legs. To make me come. To make me scream his name.

I hadn't realized I'd said the last part out loud until he chuckled and all but purred, "Oh, I'll make you come, C. I'll make you come until you see stars. You know I can."

He was right. He could. He had, many, many times before. Almost dizzy with lust at his words and the memories they evoked, I simply moaned. Reaching up to grab his wrist, I pushed it down between my legs and looked up into his eyes, silently begging him to see his promise through. His baby blues took on a gleeful look as he hooked his fingers around the crotch of my thong and pulled it to one side.

We continued to gaze at one another as he delved between my

pussy lips, already soaked with my juices, and sought my clit. It wasn't difficult to find, throbbing and desperate for attention as it was. I writhed as he touched me there, eliciting a throaty chuckle from him. He continued to watch my face as he slowly, gently, circled the sensitive bud, silently daring me to close my eyes. We'd played this game many a time in the past. He'd tease me as he watched my face, and I had to keep my eyes open, otherwise he'd stop.

I stared back at him almost insolently, biting my lip as I felt my orgasm approach. Phil moved the tips of his fingers faster and harder, and soon I felt as though my body were an elastic band, being wound tighter and tighter until it was almost painful. I begged for release.

"P-please."

"Please what, C?"

"Please, make me come." My voice was little more than a whisper.

"Well, since you asked me so nicely..."

With that, he pinched my clit, sending me tumbling into a state of screaming orgasmic bliss so loud that I was surprised the crowd in the mess didn't come rushing over to see who was being murdered. By now, I'd grabbed his shoulders to steady myself, and my fingernails dug into the taut muscles there, making him wince. I'd long since forgotten about keeping my eyes open; my hormones were much stronger than my willpower, and all I could think about was how good it felt and how much I wanted to do it again.

I'd barely cracked my eyes open when there was a flurry of movement from Phil. He stepped back and shoved a hand into the pocket of his jeans and retrieved his wallet. Clumsy in his haste, he dropped it once before retrieving it and fishing a condom out of its depths. I grinned lazily as he tossed his wallet onto a nearby table and made short work of undoing his pants. Releasing his cock from his underwear, he quickly tore into the foil packet, which he also dropped onto the table, then rolled the latex sheath down his length.

"Fuck, C, I can't wait. I have to be inside you. Now."

He looked at me questioningly and I gave a nod. He lifted me so my legs were wrapped around his back, then I leaned back against the door and slipped my hand between our bodies to move my knickers aside and guide the tip of his cock to my slick entrance. Once satisfied it was going nowhere but deep inside me, I slipped my arms around Phil's neck and lowered myself onto him.

Our moans filled the room as he filled me. Giving me a couple of seconds to adjust, he began to thrust inside me, his pubic bone slapping against my clit with each movement. I buried my face in the crook of his neck and held on for dear life as his powerful body catapulted us both to heaven. Before long, I felt his entire body stiffen and I knew what was coming. Moving my head slightly, I whispered into his ear.

"Come for me, baby."

He needed no more prompting than that. His cock leapt and spurted inside me, and an almighty yell issued from his kiss-swollen lips. His fingers dug tightly into my ass, sending a wave of tremors through my pussy. We groaned together then, panting. Phil carried me over to the table where he'd put his wallet and gently lowered me onto it. Grasping the base of the condom, he pulled out of me.

"Fuck, C," he said, looking at me with an expression of total awe. "That was incredible."

I nodded, not trusting myself to speak. I simply didn't know where to start.

Phil's brain was obviously working on the same problem as

he disposed of the condom. He continued to look at me, then a little crease appeared between his eyebrows.

Moving to sit on the table beside me, he took my hands in his and said, "Christina. We've both fucked up, all right? I know it was mainly my fault, so I'll allow you to hold it against me for the rest of my life, but I love you. I'm not saying it won't be tough, but I'd rather have it tough *with* you than easy *without* you. What do you say?"

"I say we've got an awful lot to talk about, but yes. I love you, too, and right now, that's all that matters."

He squeezed me tightly and I hugged him back, scarcely believing that the man I'd never stopped loving was back in my arms. Reality intruded and I pulled away from him and began to straighten myself out.

"So, what now?" Phil said, moving to make himself presentable again as well.

Realizing how long we'd been away, I smiled wryly. "Right now, I think we've got some explaining to do."

AGAINST THE WALL

Catherine Paulssen

The humming of a building crane and monotonous strike of a distant hammer beat heavily through the idleness of the summer afternoon as Annie let her eyes wander over the groups of soldiers lingering across from her perch on the watchtower—the men from the 8th Infantry Division on her side of the barbed wire and slabs of concrete, the Russian soldiers gathering with members of the East German police corps on the other.

None of them seemed to have anything particular to do. They looked as calm as the air that hung leaden over the city. But she knew the soldiers on West Berlin ground had a sharp eye on what was happening on the other side of the border, which would soon be manifested with a wall much taller than a man's height. They were watching the enemy, on the lookout for even the slightest commotion that could be a sign of people trying to escape to freedom.

The Soviet soldiers who guarded the construction site on the eastern side were looking for the exact same thing.

Two weeks ago, they had started to build the wall, and ever since that day, fugitives had been fleeing the eastern part of the city. Officially, the U.S. troops and the Allied forces stationed around them didn't interfere. But it was an open secret that they would help anyone who made an attempt to choose their side.

Annie sighed. Even though the soldiers appeared to have hardly anything to do, she would have traded her work as a cryptographer any time for their tasks. She had never been one for staying inside, and she would happily have exchanged her uniform and pumps for her male comrades' boots and fatigues. She scratched her neck, sticky with a sheen of sweat. At least the skirt was a welcome relief for one of the hottest summers Europe had seen in decades.

She reached for a field glass and let her gaze wander over the Soviet soldiers leaning against a fence. They all looked the same to her. Tall and pale-skinned, but with red cheeks and a slightly defiant, proud expression around their lips. One, though, stood out from the crowd. His stout figure gave him an authoritative appearance but his gestures when he talked weren't stodgy or gruff at all. His face was round and open.

She would sometimes catch sight of him on her strolls outside the command post, and her heart would always beat a bit faster, though she couldn't exactly figure out why. He wasn't supposed to make her feel that way, after all. She was a county commissioner's daughter from the Midwest; she believed in the Apollo mission, Elvis Presley and the New York Yankees.

He was a captain serving a communist regime.

He took off his cap and wiped his forehead. She adjusted the binocular to take a closer look. His light blond hair was just a bit too long. Not so much that it would get him into trouble with regulations, but enough for her to notice. She imagined him losing himself in tunes played by forbidden radio stations as soon as his daily duty was over.

"Second Lieutenant McMillan," came a voice behind her. She turned and saluted the first lieutenant. "Keeping a close watch on the enemy?"

"I..."

"You know you're not supposed to be up here," he said. His voice was stern, but she could see an amused glimmer in his eyes.

"I'm sorry, sir, but I'm off duty."

"Even more reason," he said good-naturedly.

"Yes, sir."

That night when she went to bed in her cabin, sleep didn't find her for hours. She blamed the still, humid air, but deep down she knew the true culprit was the Soviet soldier.

"You can't go out there now!" Mae protested. "Look!" She pointed at the window, where towering gray clouds had darkened the sky so much that the late-afternoon sky looked more like evening. Thunder rolled in the distance.

"I have to. My mother gave me that watch before I left for Europe!" Annie grabbed her garrison cap and gave her friend a look that sought her understanding. "I know where I must have lost it. I'll be back before the storm gets here."

Before Mae could further object, Annie ran out of the office building that hosted their command post and headed straight for the construction line. When she reached the deserted no-man's-land, the first drops of rain began to fall. Heavy, thick blobs soon speckled the dusty ground with dark spots. She threw a glance at the clouds being chased by the wind. No way would she return now, even if the price to pay was getting soaked to the bone. She'd probably lost her watch while strolling here during lunch break today, and she silently cursed herself for not having replaced its threadbare strap earlier.

Through an opening where the barbed wire hadn't already been replaced with cement slabs, she could see some workers running into a shed and the lights being turned on in the Russian barracks. The machines stood still and all she could hear was the thunder's glowering rumble. She passed a pile of cobblestones that smelled as only stones could in the middle of a city when the summer rain made their smooth surface shine.

Careful not to come too close to the fence while keeping her eyes on the ground, she startled when a bolt of lightning tore through the gloom. Thunder followed a moment later, hard and striking, piercing the air with its force. As if on command, the raindrops multiplied. Soon enough, her cord jacket was soggy, and she could feel the wetness soaking her shirt. She turned up the collar of the jacket to prevent streaks of water from trickling down her wet hair onto her neck.

Big puddles formed on the ground. She hadn't expected them to cover the site that quickly, but suddenly, she found herself in the middle of a vast lake with only a few islands of mud scattered across it. She stuffed her cap into the pocket of her jacket and started to jump from dry spot to dry spot, unable to see much ahead of her, so thick was the curtain of water lashing down. Realizing she had come quite close to the wall, she paused and looked for a place to wait for the thunderstorm to pass. Suddenly, she felt a hand grabbing her shoulder. She shrieked and turned to find the bearlike Soviet soldier standing right next to her.

"*Nje*," he said, making a gesture with his fingers, then pointing to where they were standing. She looked at him with wide eyes, and he added the word "*Gefahr*," his voice loud to drown out the rushing of the wind and water.

She thought she knew the meaning of that German word. "You mean it's dangerous to be here?"

He nodded. "Dangerous."

His accent was hard, but it was softened by the concern in his voice. She ducked her head as another flash of lightning darted from above. "But there's no one around and I know the area."

Did she see his mouth twitch in the dazzling white light? He said something in Russian, then shook his head. "Woman *nje* out. Dangerous."

"I'm not a woman. I'm a second lieutenant in the Women's Army Corps of the United States of America." She raised her chin and tried her best not to blink as the raindrops hit her eyes.

He frowned and she wondered if he suddenly realized that she was, after all, the enemy. But then he broke out in loud laughter, a laughter so hearty, it couldn't be swallowed even by the grumbling thunder.

"Come," he said curtly.

He grabbed her arm and rushed her across the open space to a place where concrete slabs were piled high. As she tried to keep up with his long steps, she wondered if it was wise to follow a Soviet soldier with nobody in her unit knowing where she was. And yet, this was more a curious feeling than real fear.

At one side of the piled slabs stood a small stand where cigarette stubs swam in big pools of rainwater. He dragged her behind it to a narrow passageway where the stand's roof met the stacked slabs. It was dry, and the cement had even stored some of the day's heat.

Annie leaned against the back of the shelter and smiled at him. "Thank you."

He returned the smile. He pointed to his chest. "Sergei."

Her smile became bigger. "I'm Annie."

He nodded formally, and she couldn't help but finding him incredibly endearing.

Now, no longer running or concentrating on her way, she

became aware of how the water had crept into every layer of her clothing and how chilly she was. Sergei took off the raincoat he was wearing. He folded it, carefully laid it on the floor and took off his jacket as well. Another thunderbolt lightened the darkness for a few seconds, and she could see that he had not been affected much by the rain apart from a few dark patches on his shoulders.

He took a step toward her and motioned her to take off her jacket. She could feel his eyes on her face as she unbuttoned it, and it made the blood rush to her cheeks. Her fingers trembled, and she fumbled with the buttons. He waited patiently, then took the damp cord suit jacket from her hands and placed it on top of his coat. She could smell his body and the rain as he reached around her to put his jacket over her shoulders. In the mingling scents of wet cord, gabardine, rain-soaked mud and his soap, she felt strangely comforted and safe. He closed the top button of the jacket, and Annie could feel the goose bumps vanishing from her cold skin.

"Thank you," she said once more and cleared her throat as she heard her own voice croaky and strange.

"*Spahseeba,*" he said, and his breath touched her face. It smelled of tea and some fruit, dark and sweet.

"*Spahseeba?*"

"Thank you. *Russki.*"

"Oh." She blushed and tugged the coat a bit closer around her. He didn't retreat; instead, he propped one of his huge hands against the wall and continued to watch her.

Annie raised her head a bit and looked directly into his face. "*Spahseeba,*" she whispered, and the next moment, the fruity smell of his breath touched her lips, followed by his warm mouth on hers.

Another flash of light streaked through the passageway, and

by the time the thunder roared, he had pressed her against the shelter's wall. She grabbed his arms, and they felt just as strong as she'd imagined they would.

He lifted her up a little while he kissed her, and for a moment she could feel how excited he was beneath his uniform pants. They broke the kiss, and even in the shadows she could see the quizzical look on his face.

She bit her bottom lip and took off his cap. His hands didn't let go of her waist, and they radiated warmth to her skin even through her damp shirt. He stood completely still. She ran her fingers through the blond hair and down his temple. When he didn't show any reaction, she traced the shape of his lips with her fingertip. He opened them, and she ran her fingers farther down his chin, over his neck, to the hollow above his collarbone. She pressed herself a little closer against him and placed a kiss on his mouth.

The force with which he answered and deepened her kiss left no doubt that he had just been waiting for her cue. The tenderness of his hands as they crept underneath her shirt to explore her skin revealed that it hadn't been a lack of experience or shyness holding him back. A shiver ran through her body as his rough fingers stroked down her spine to the waistband of her skirt. She moaned softly into his mouth as his hands followed the line of her curves from her hips up to her breasts. He smiled against her lips and cupped her breast, caressing it gently.

Another flash lit up the sky, and she noticed that it took a while until the thunder followed. The rain was still pouring, but she couldn't help feeling anxious—anxious that the workers would return, anxious that someone might catch them redhanded. She fumbled with the buttons of his pants, and he stepped back a bit. While she opened his slacks, he watched her face, his gaze unwavering.

"U tebya krahseeviyeh glahza," he muttered. The admiration in his eyes told her something about the meaning of the mysterious words, and when his thumb ran over her brow and down her cheek, she assumed he had given her a compliment about her looks.

She gave him a smile as she found her way into his shorts and fondled him. It was arousing her almost as much as him. His cock bobbed against her hand, and she curled her fingers around it. He closed his eyes and groaned. Very softly, she began stroking him up and down, and he let her do as she pleased for some moments. Then, with the next rumble that rolled through the skies, Annie found herself pinned against the wall of the shelter. Maybe he was realizing that the thunderstorm wouldn't last much longer; maybe her caress had become too much.

Maybe he had wanted her all along.

He shoved up her skirt and yanked down her panties. A strangled moan escaped his lips as his fingers stroked her pussy, and the surprise she thought she heard left her embarrassed by how aroused she was. She lowered her gaze. Sergei lifted up her chin. The look in his eyes was sincere, and the kiss he gave her made her abandon any feelings of shame.

He took the hand that was still rubbing his cock and put it around his neck. He held her tight as he entered her carefully, but when she responded to his first deliberate strokes, he grew more daring. Her fingers dug into his shoulder and a surge of warmth flooded her body as he completely abandoned his restraint. Annie buried her face in his chest as he rocked her with heavy thrusts.

Their moans mixed with the sound of raindrops tumbling on the roof and the hauling of the wind around their retreat. A bolt of light flashed through the clouds, and as the thunder died in the distance, they leaned against each other, gasping. Her head rested against Sergei's heaving chest and she drank in his scent.

He didn't break away immediately, but rocked her a little bit back and forth in his arms, as if he were dancing to a tune playing in his head.

"Sergei..." she whispered, and he smiled. He placed two fingers on her mouth, then moved them to his mouth and kissed the tips that had just touched her lips.

After he had refastened his clothes, he bent down and picked up her jacket. In a silent gesture, he held it out to her, but instead of taking it, she wrapped her arms around him and remained in his embrace until the rain's intensity was no more than a soft thrum on the roof.

"If I stay for much longer, I won't be able to leave," she whispered, and she knew he understood because his arms held her even tighter, and he buried his face in her hair.

"I will see you again one day," he said, determination in his gruff voice.

She took her jacket from his hands, removed his coat and reached around him to drape it around his shoulders. *"Spahseeba,"* she whispered and quickly kissed him.

She hopped through the muddy pools back to her command post, not noticing the water that splashed across her legs or how the construction site was once again filling up with workers. Only when she reached the security booth did she throw a quick glance back.

Her watch would be forever gone. But she had found something else while searching for it.

A few days later, as she was on her way out of the office, Annie passed a group of fellow soldiers from her unit talking about the Russian troops. She bent over the water fountain to listen.

"I heard it is some sick sort of sport to them, like a...a hunt," she overheard one of the women saying.

"And afterward, they brag about how they seduced the enemy," another woman said.

Annie choked on the water she was about to swallow and ran for the bathroom, where she threw up. She stared at her pale face in the mirror, eyes red-rimmed with suppressed sadness.

So he was one of those? No, he couldn't be. He had treated her with such respect and consideration. She rinsed her mouth to get rid of the sickening taste.

The doubts didn't leave her all day, and they continued to haunt her deep into the night. By lunch break the next day, she had decided she would take the risk of climbing up the watchtower again. She wasn't sure what she expected to see or if it even mattered at all.

She saluted the guard on duty and, when he didn't pay her much attention, walked past him toward the side of the tower facing the border.

There he was—Sergei, standing in a group of soldiers patrolling the construction site. She watched him turn to a private and strike up a chat. Something the private said must have been funny because soon Sergei was laughing. As she watched his open mouth she remembered the sound of his laughter, deep and genuine. The other soldier walked away and Sergei turned his head toward where she was standing.

He squinted and stood completely still.

She held her breath as she watched him cast a quick glance around before looking back right at her. His face crinkled into a broad, authentic smile, and for the blink of a second, he tipped his hat.

In the bright midday sun, she smiled back at him. One day.

THE THUNDER
OF WAR

Anya Richards

He dreamed of her, the need so great it gave excruciating reality to every sensation, burning them into his skin. Every imagined sound echoed through his soul, taking him home.

Beautiful Mei, her slim body curled around his side, the weight of her thick black hair spread over his chest, a few strands fanning up to feather his cheek. He traced the gentle valley of her spine, curled his fingers around her hip to softly explore the sleek skin stretched taut across the bone. Even caught in the grip of deep sleep she moved closer, the leg thrown over his thighs tightening and a sigh whispering from her to warm him all the way through.

Holding his breath so as to better feel the rise and fall of her rib cage, he treasured the memory of each inhalation, the little rush of each exhale. Her body was so slight, seemed too tiny to contain the lioness spirit he so loved, surely too small to bear the weight of his desire. Sometimes he felt like a brute when his body covered hers, the contrast between his hulking frame and her slender beauty never more marked than then. But her arms always welcomed him, her eyes encouraging every intimacy, no matter how rough. Mei would wrap her legs around his waist and pulled him deeper, urging him to *hurry, hurry* and give her all he had.

Sometimes she would push him onto his back, hands firm with determination as she mounted him, taking him in one frantic plunge. As she rocked and swiveled, her prim little mouth would whisper how much she loved the feel of his hardness stretching her, how much he turned her on.

Did she realize that when they made love, just being with her filled him more completely than his cock ever filled her sweet, wet pussy?

Body growing taut with remembered ecstasy, he cupped the firmness of her ass softly, not wanting to wake her. The cheek fit perfectly into his palm, and he imagined letting his hand fall lower, fingers creeping between her parted thighs and over the soft strands of hair, finding them damp with anticipation. He'd explore her slowly with only the lightest touches, intentionally making her crazy. Soon she'd be pressing against his hand, those little whimpers that wordlessly begged for more breaking from her throat and driving him insane in return.

The background of his mind—the part that never really slept but constantly patrolled—went on alert, making him suddenly aware of the heat pressing down on him, sealing him to the bed with a slick of sweat. A rumble sounded in the distance, accompanied by a staccato rattle, like hail on the roof.

Not thunder and hail—explosions and gunfire.

Anger gripped him that the sounds of conflict should intrude on his memories of her. The two things didn't belong in his brain at the same time, should never come in contact, even remotely. That was why he fought, put his life on the line so that Mei

and their kids would never have to live with the constant fear
of violence, never lie in bed and hear bombs going off down the
road. Even her dream presence at such a time was an abomina-
tion to everything he stood for. It made the steel in him harden,
grow cold with rage.

Shh...

He tried to ignore her voice, push Mei aside and lock her
back into the recesses of his mind where the horrors of Afghanistan, in the throes of its deadly struggles, couldn't touch her,
even in his imagination.

She wouldn't go.

Instead her hand, now pressed over his heart, was warmer
than the sultry air, and the brush of her lips against his chest
was more real than the hardness of the cot beneath him.

It's all right, darling. Mei's fingers circled, rubbing with
soothing intent. *Let go.*

Any moment now the siren would go off, ripping him out of
his dream and into action. Instinctively he squeezed her tighter
than he ever would have had she really been in his arms. In his
dreams he didn't have to temper his strength.

Yes, darling. He couldn't decide if she sounded sad or merely
winded from the hug. *Hang on to me.*

But conversely her words made him loosen his hold. She
tightened hers on him instead.

"They're gonna need me. Any minute now they'll sound the
muster."

She lifted up on one elbow, and her breath fanned his cheek
as she said, "Stay here with me until they do, Jack."

He couldn't refuse her anything. She knew it too, but never
asked for the impossible or more than he could give without
surrendering his soul. It was one of the things he loved most
about her. He knew the life he offered wasn't what she would

have chosen for herself, wasn't anywhere near ideal. Hell, she'd given birth to Donny alone but never once blamed him for it. When he brought it up she just shrugged and reminded him that she'd known who and what he was from the beginning. That on their first date he'd told her he was a lifer—army to the core.

It was something he needed—the knowledge of being a part of something bigger, more important than himself, of being of service to others in a fundamental way. Once he met her a new dimension had opened in his life, one he never wanted to lose, but a life of service wasn't always compatible with having a relationship. Sometimes, even now, he wondered if it could really last. Then he'd look into her eyes, see the unwavering acceptance, and fall for her all over again. Her refusal to make him choose between duty and love chained him to her with an unbreakable bond.

The rumble of conflict still sounded, now accompanied with the thud of booted feet and the roar of engines firing up. He should be out there. Who knew what was happening, which of his comrades might be hurt, in need of reinforcement? Yet longing to give in to her plea made him hesitate.

As though sensing his indecision, she whispered, "Stay, until they come to get you."

So he subsided onto the cot, sank back into the dream, even while still listening to the hellish sounds of the outside world. But they were fading slightly, ceding to the strength of his need for just a little more time to dream of home.

"Ah, Jack. My Jack."

Mei touched her lips to his so softly, so swiftly he had no time to respond. Then her mouth drifted lower, all the way to his chest, and he caught his breath. He exhaled with a groan when her teeth grazed his nipple.

The thunder grew louder, and Jack tensed.

"No, my darling." Warm air blew across his abs as she spoke, and the stress of combat was instantly transmuted to coiled desire. "They haven't come yet. Stay."

"Mei." He couldn't let the fantasy continue. It was the worst possible time to be lost in her enchantment. Tangling his fingers into her hair, he tried to hold her still. "I have to go."

But not even ten years of army discipline could help him when she whispered once more, "Stay," and touched her tongue to the tip of his cock.

"Oh god."

Squeezing his eyes even tighter shut, he gave in to the wet heat of her mouth moving slowly, gloriously over his flesh. In repose it was such a prudish-looking mouth, with thin, solemn lips and slightly downturned corners. Even when Mei smiled it was usually with a quality of restraint that brought to mind schoolteachers and librarians. But when she sucked him—oh, god, when she sucked him—the slip of her tongue, the ravenous way she surrounded his cock, gave lie to those impressions.

And the memory of looking down, seeing that proper little mouth opening, taking him in, always shot his arousal into the stratosphere. Remembering the way she wriggled and moaned, with pleasure in what she was doing evident in every move and sound, drove him crazy.

But she was forcing him to the edge of orgasm too quickly, the suction of her mouth and the play of her hand on his balls making him arch up to meet her every downward plunge.

He pulled her away, groaning as she pressed against his hands, obviously wanting to go back to what she was doing.

"Let me love you, Jack."

He shuddered. Those were his favorite words in the world. A bomb could fall on his tent killing him instantly and he would die happy with his last memory being her saying that.

Without replying he pulled her up and over so she draped across his chest, and took her lips, inhaling her breath, trying to steal her soul the way she'd stolen his. Mei opened her mouth for him, welcomed him with a sound of such need his balls drew up tight and his arousal went from insistent to desperate. Yet the kiss was sweet—filled with desire but not frantic—all soft sweeps and tangles of tongues, breathy moans.

The slight weight of her body on his was perfection. Her warmth and scent soaked into his pores until his entire world once more shrank to her—only her.

He couldn't stop his hands from moving, reveling in the sleek skin, delicate muscles and sinuous motions of her body, her back and arms, nape and shoulders, buttocks and thighs. Getting lost in her was so damn easy. Sliding his lips across her cheek, he aimed for the sensitive spot behind her ear, but she turned her head, following his motion.

"Jack," she whispered against his mouth. "Kiss me more. Don't stop."

Nothing. He could deny her nothing. So he lifted the fraction necessary and gave her his heart once more through his kiss. Mei took it, as she always did, and the caressing motion of her lips said she would always keep it safe.

But he wanted more—needed more—yearning blasting over him like the wash of a jet engine on takeoff. Reaching between her thighs to find the slick, wet flesh, he teased her clit with a butterfly stroke, was rewarded by her gasp, the trembling of her thighs as they gripped his waist. Suddenly her gentleness disappeared and he felt the lioness awake. Little growls of pleasure rumbled from her throat as she nipped at his tongue and lower lip, and her fingers dug almost painfully into his biceps. She pressed down, trying to increase the contact with his finger, but he locked his arm around her waist and held her in place.

She was so hot and wet, slick as drenched satin. It always thrilled him to know he could do this to her, bring out her desires with nothing more than kisses and the love that boiled fierce beneath his skin. With more light strokes he tormented her, knowing the gentle exploration wasn't what she wanted. Slowly he slipped the tip of his finger into her, just up to the first knuckle, feeling her inner muscles clamp down, try to pull it farther in. When he withdrew, the sound she made into his mouth was feral, and he couldn't help his huff of laughter.

Finally breaking the kiss he pushed her to sit up, straddling his abdomen. Mei tried to slide back, intent on getting his cock into her, but he gripped her hips hard and held her still.

"Jack." Her voice cracked slightly, and the sound of it made his cock pulse.

"Hold on, baby." He slid one hand up to cover a breast, heard her gasping exhalation when he tweaked the tight nipple between his index and middle fingers. "Give me a little more time."

Arching her back pushed her breast farther into his palm. "All the time you want."

Her breasts were so sensitive, so responsive. With a couple of pinches the nipples were as tight as they could be and she was panting, the instinctive jerking of her hips leaving a slick, wet trail on his stomach. When he curled up and took one furled peak into his mouth, Mei held on to his head and cried out his name again.

Inch by inch he licked, sucked and nipped all around the small mounds, worshiping the tender skin.

"Oh God, Jack." She was rubbing her pussy against him, harder and harder, with jerky, shuddering motions. "I want you so bad."

Dropping back against the pillow, he lifted her effortlessly, bringing her pussy up toward his lips. Mei kept her grip on his head and settled over his face with a little moan, spreading her legs, bracing her knees on the pillow.

He didn't know why, but this position always made him feel vulnerable, as though the pinning of his head to the bed with her body and muffling of his hearing by her thighs put him at a disadvantage. For a man not used to feeling in any way helpless, it was an almost claustrophobic sensation that brought with it a jagged stab of fear. She was the only one he would let shackle him this way, and the knowledge of that truth only heightened his enjoyment.

Sometimes he let her set the pace, but this was his dream, and he didn't give her that opportunity. Gripping her ass, he brought her into full contact with his mouth, held her there as he swept his tongue from the entrance of her pussy up to her clitoris. Opening his mouth as wide as he could, creating suction, he tried to drink her, eat her whole. The taste of her, her scent and the sensation of her slick folds on his tongue always drove him wild. He couldn't get enough. Over and over he lashed at her pulsing flesh until he heard from her rhythmic, escalating cries that she was close to coming.

Closing his lips over her clit, lashing and sucking, he took her over the edge. Mei tensed and bowed, nails digging into his scalp, and the wild, high sound of her release almost made him lose his mind. Her hips jerked, making him tighten his grip on her ass so as to keep contact with the pulsing flesh. She tried to pull away, but he wouldn't let her. He wanted more—more of her scent inundating his head, more of her taste filling his mouth—more of her heart-shaking pleasure at his touch.

Pressing his tongue flat to her clitoris, forcing himself not to move, he gentled her, yet kept her simmering just at the boundary of arousal. The rhythm of Mei's orgasmic contractions slowed, her body relaxed in his hands. But her breathing was still ragged, and her hips began to move in a subtle, circular motion, telling him she was once more climbing toward ecstasy.

Easing her body up slightly so as to slick his tongue through her folds, he lapped slowly, resisting the urge to lash her to another quick orgasm. He loved making her come over and over, always wanted to leave her limp and completely spent at the end.

She was mewling, pressing down against his hands, obviously wanting him to go faster, harder. But he ignored her demands, taking his time, circling her hole, caressing the smooth skin behind it, tickling over her hard little clit. Once more her nails scraped his scalp, her thighs tightened on either side of his head. The speed with which she was again scaling the wall of pleasure made his cock pulse in sympathetic desperation.

"Jack," she cried, her need echoing between them. "Oh, Jack, you're making me crazy."

She wasn't alone. He couldn't take much more either. But this time he wanted to watch her come, needed to see her porcelain skin flush pink and damp with desire, watch her face contort and her lips part as she panted and cried out. And there was always a moment when she opened her eyes and looked at him with a glazed, almost surprised expression, as though she couldn't believe what she was feeling. He lived for those moments, for the instinctive, love-filled smile she gave him just before she reached her peak. Then, just for that split second, he truly felt like a hero—her hero—and life was complete, perfect.

With one swift movement he rolled her onto her back. Leaning over her, he absorbed her heavy-lidded eyes, the way her lips appeared slightly puffy from his kisses, the rosy glow that suffused her cheeks, neck and chest. She held out her arms, opened her legs and tilted her hips up, inviting him to do what they both so urgently wanted.

Sound boomed through the tent, and he started to roll away, tried to shake himself out of the dream. He'd been so into it he felt disoriented, couldn't tell whether what he'd heard was a bomb, mortar or tank fire. He had to go, throw on his fatigues and get out there. Why hadn't the muster sounded? Why hadn't someone come for him?

He was struggling to get off his cot, realized something was wrapped around his chest, holding him back.

"No, Jack. It's just thunder, baby."

He shook his head, trying to dispel the lingering sense of unreality. It sounded so much like Mei, as though she was really there. But she wasn't, couldn't be. His brain insisted he fight to get free, get out and do his job, but his body wouldn't listen. Not even in the grip of a hallucination would he risk hurting Mei. Adrenaline pumped through his system, driving his heart rate to maximum speed, making his muscles twitch with the need to move, to battle his way through to the other side—back to sanity.

"Sweetheart, please. Look at me." A soft hand pressed to his cheek, trying to force his head around. "Jack, you're home. You're with me."

"No." He shook his head, realized his eyes were closed, didn't want to force them open and see that it really had all been a dream. "No. I have to go. They need me."

"I need you too, Jack. Let me have you now. Please?"

It was the sound of tears in her voice that made him open his eyes and turn his head to look, although now he knew for sure it must be just a dream.

Mei never cried.

But she was weeping now, dark eyes wide, rivulets of tears

streaking her cheeks. Jack blinked, shook his head to clear his suddenly blurred vision, his stomach clenching with anguish. Unable to maintain contact with her shadowed gaze, he let his slip around the room. It was their bedroom. The bed they were on was the one they'd bought together just before they married. The dark shapes of the dresser and rocking chair were familiar in the gloom. Even unable to see them, he knew exactly where the pictures of the kids were on the wall and that the darker square on the bedside table was the wedding picture of Mei and him. The sheer curtains at the window fluttered in the breeze, and he knew he'd lifted the sash just a little before bed, as he did every warm night.

Lightning lit the room and was followed a few seconds later by a crack of thunder. Jack winced. Mei's arms tightened around his chest.

"I'm sorry." He'd never had trouble apologizing before, but now the words stuck in his throat, trapped by shame and fear. Coming home, getting back into the family routine and relaxing his guard was never easy, but this was different. He could have hurt her....

"Jesus." He lunged to turn on the bedside light. When he twisted back toward her, the shock on her face made him pause, but only for a moment. He wanted to cup her cheek, check every inch of her skin for bruises, but he hesitated, not knowing how she would react. His hand, suspended between them, was shaking, his heart pounded in his throat. "Did I hurt you?"

"No!" Mei clasped her fingers around his and pressed his palm to her chest, right above her heart. "You would never hurt me, Jack."

He wished he had her certainty, tried to bring his dream into focus so as to know for himself whether she was telling the truth. But it was all a blur. "Are you sure?"

"Positive." She feathered her fingertip over his cheek to his lips. When she traced back and forth across the lower one, a shudder tripped down his spine. "You blew my mind." A little frown wrinkled her brow and she glanced down for a moment. When she lifted her gaze back to his, determination firmed her lips. "I just wish it hadn't all been part of a dream—a nightmare—for you."

He couldn't deny it—hated that he couldn't—but he also couldn't let her think of it that way. In the army they taught you not to let small problems become big ones, to deal with things immediately so no one got hurt. Risking her rejection, he reached for her, sighed with relief when she came to him willingly, eagerly, like she always had.

"It wasn't a nightmare, Mei." Gently settling her back on the bed, he leaned over her, giving himself permission to caress her torso until his hand came to rest on her breast. Her nipple immediately began to tighten and he couldn't resist playing with it, rolling it slowly until it became a stiff peak once more. She drew in her breath with a little hiss, her eyelids drooping slightly, and he felt the tension in his gut ease a little more.

"When we're apart, thoughts and dreams of you keep me sane." Bending, he pressed a soft kiss to her solemn lips, spoke against them. "I remember everything about you—the way you look coming out of the shower or brushing your hair, cooking, cuddling with the children—everything. I lie in bed pulling out memories and playing them in my head like movies, hurting and longing just to see you. And when I come home, it's as though my brain can't quite accept that I'm back and keeps doing the same thing, thinking of you, longing for you, even though you're right beside me."

The tip of her tongue swept his lower lip, and she lifted her arms to twine around his neck, one hand sweeping down his back, the other curling around his nape. "So all we did are things you dream of doing to me while you're away?"

"Those and more." He inhaled sharply as her palm slid around to his groin, her fingers finding his cock and bringing it back to full erection with just a light touch. "You know I have a really good memory."

Her little laugh, the slow pump of her hand, brought the fire back to raging life under his skin. Following her lead, he cupped her mound, parting her pussy lips and sinking his fingers into her heat. The instinctive upward jerk of her hips, the parting of her thighs to give him full access, caused a rush of desire so powerful it made his head spin.

"What do you think you'd have dreamed next?"

Jack rolled on top of her, settling between her thighs, both of them moving with the ease of long, satisfying practice so that his cock was immediately perfectly positioned.

"I'm sure this was it." He sank into her slowly, gritting his teeth against the intense pleasure of having his hardness surrounded, welcomed by her slick, hot walls. Holding back when all he wanted to do was thrust them both to orgasmic oblivion. "I wanted to watch you come. I need that so much."

Mei moaned, closed her eyes. Soon she was panting and whispering how much she loved to feel his cock inside her, how hard he was, how close she was to coming. So delicious to hear such dirty words from that prissy little mouth again, and the sight and sound sharpened his need until it bit at his belly, gathered like a conflagration in his veins. Jack kept his movements long and powerful, the way she liked them. A flush rose to stain her cheeks again and her pussy clasped him, the contractions getting faster and stronger as she rocketed toward climax.

Suddenly her eyes popped open and the look she gave him, filled with love, overwhelming passion and that funny, adorable hint of surprise, made his heart swell. The heat in his groin coalesced, dropped into his balls and pushed him into orgasm just as she cried out, her pussy milking his cock until he thought he'd pass out from the pleasure.

As he rolled over, pulling her against his side once more, he wanted her to understand. He wasn't good with words or emotions, but she needed to know. So he tilted her head up to look at her and whispered, "You're home to me, Mei; home and peace and sanity. I can do anything when I know you love me."

Then he kissed her once more. Her answer came in the sweetness of her response, the tightness of her arms holding him as close as possible. Outside, the storm moved farther away and sounds of war retreated from his dreams.

SERGEANT RAE

Sacchi Green

Sgt. Rae was so strong she could carry me at a run through gunfire and smoke and exploding mines. Two years later, she's that strong again. With just one hand she can hold me from getting away, no matter how hard I struggle. Even her voice is enough to stop me at a dead run, so it doesn't matter that she can't run anymore. And anyway, I'd never want to run away.

I'm smaller, but I've got my own kind of muscle even if it doesn't show. A mechanic in an armored tank unit has to be strong just to handle the tools you need, and if you're a woman doing the job you need a whole extra layer of strength. I'm not an army mechanic anymore, but I can still use tools; Sgt. Rae isn't an army sergeant any more, but she'll always be in charge. At the town hall where she's the police and fire department dispatcher, they tell me she's got the whole place organized like it's never been before.

In our house or in town, I'm supposed to just call her Rae these days, and mostly I remember. I'm just Jenny. In the bedroom, we don't need names at all except to wake each other when the bad dreams come and whisper that everything's all right now. Or close enough to handle, as long as we're together.

Out here on this trail I've made through the woods and across the stream, we play by my rules, and that means I'm Specialist 2nd Brown and she's the ball-buster staff sergeant, even though neither of us has any use for balls.

She'll be coming along the trail behind me any minute, coming to see what new contraption I've constructed. What she expects is something like the exercise stations I've built for her into every room in the house, chinning bars and railings and handgrips at different levels, and in a way that's right, but with a different twist. She expects I'll want her to order me to drop and do fifty push-ups or sit-ups, or run in place until I'm panting, but this time I want more.

I check the gears and pulleys one more time, even though I already know the tension is set right. It's my own tension that's nearly out of control. The posts and crossbars are rock-solid while I'm shaking in my old fatigues, so nervous and horny that I can't even tell which is which.

I hear the motor now. I could've made it run quieter, but if you've been where I've been, where we've both been, you want to be sure you know who's coming around the bend.

She's crossed the rocky ford in the stream where no regular wheelchair could have gone. I salvaged tracks from old snow-mobiles at the repair shop where I work and they're as good as any armored tank tracks, even though they're made of Kevlar instead of steel. Fine for this terrain, and even the steel kind got chewed up in the desert sand in Iraq.

Mustn't think about the desert now. Here in New Hamp-shire, green leaves overhead are beginning to turn orange and red. This stream flows into a river just beyond our house, and we can watch canoes and kayaks pass by; no desert in sight. This is home. We're together. Safe. Except that safe isn't always enough, when you've known—had to know—so much more.

Now I hear Sgt. Rae veering back and forth through the obstacle course, steering the mini-tank around trees, stumps, boulders, right over small logs. With a double set of the tracks on each side, the only way to steer is by slowing one side while accelerating the other, and that takes strength. I think of her big hands on the levers, the bunched muscles of her arms and shoulders, even stronger now than in the army because she insists on a manually powered chair anywhere but in these woods. Gloves help, but her hands get calloused from turning the wheels. Calloused, and rough even when she tries to be gentle... Anticipation pounds through my cunt.

I kneel on the ground, close my eyes, try to clear my mind— but on the distant bridge over the river a truck backfires. In spite of the leafy dampness the desert flashes around me again, the clouds of dust, the explosions, the machine-gun fire on that final day. I think of Sgt. Rae's powerful voice, how it cut through the pain and confusion and kept me breathing when I didn't think I could last another second. "Brown!" she bellowed, again and again, coming closer to where the shattered truck cab trapped me. "Brown, damn you, report!" That sound gripped me, forced strength into me, so that I moved just a little, no matter how much it hurt, and she found me.

I never remember what happened next. I don't think Sgt. Rae does, either, but somebody told me later they found a bent assault rifle barrel nearby, and maybe she levered the truck cab up enough with that to drag me out. I just remember being slung over her shoulder, feeling her run and swerve and run some more, and hearing her voice drilling right through to my heart in a tone I'd never heard before. "Jenny, Jenny...hang on..."

Right then, with bullets still screaming around us, it was like I'd died and woken up to a new world. Ever since the day we met, Sgt. Rae had mesmerized me, obsessed me, and I'd worked to hide my foolish longings behind hard work and casual jokes and chatter. But in that moment, as her strong voice shook, a window opened in the midst of hell and gave me a glimpse of a heaven better than anything they'd ever preached about in church.

I passed out when she set me down behind a sand bunker some of our guys had piled up in a hurry. Maybe I heard somebody say another soldier was still out there, or maybe I just heard later how she went back into that hell. Either way, I know she went.

It was a month before I saw Sgt. Rae again. I was still bandaged, but up and walking. She wasn't. At first, when I stood beside the hospital bed, I wondered whether she was really there at all until she saw me.

"Jenny?"

I could scarcely hear the word. But then strength came back into her voice, and the power I'd always felt surrounding her was there again as though a light had been switched on. "Specialist Brown, report!"

So I did, listing my injuries and treatments and recovery, even though her half smile softened the formal order. Later, when she'd had her meds and fallen asleep, I pumped the nurses about her injuries and prognosis, and from that day I was never away from her for more than a few hours. There were some rough parts, and sometimes I had to be the strong one to get her through. A nurse or two caught on that there was more to it than just that she'd saved my life, but they never made any fuss. It helped that I could fix mechanical glitches in the orthopedic ward's equipment and even make some things work better than originally designed; I think somewhere along the line they claimed me as an adjunct physical therapy technician.

The dampness of the ground soaking through my jeans brings me back to the present. Sgt. Rae is coming around the clump of hemlock saplings. It's time and now I'm ready, in position, on my knees, hands clasped high above my head, ropes wrapped around my wrists, head bowed.

"Brown!"

I can't salute in this position, but I try to sound as though I were doing it. "Sergeant, yes Sergeant!"

"What do you think you're doing, Brown?"

"Sergeant, I'm kneeling, Sergeant."

"I can see that. But do you *know* what you're doing?"

Without looking I can tell she's surveying the situation. A pair of leather-wrapped rings hangs right where she can stretch up and reach them. The system of gears and pulleys is rigged to offer just the right amount of resistance and stability for her to pull herself to a standing position, brace with forearms at chest level on a crossbar, and then lower her weight slowly back down. Three of the doorways in our house have similar setups, but this one is more complex—and in this one, the counterweight is me.

"Sergeant, yes Sergeant, I do know what I'm doing."

There's the slightest of creaks as she begins to rise. The ropes tighten, and I rise, too, until I'm dangling in the air, helpless—or as helpless as I can make myself seem. My wrists are padded just enough to keep the circulation from being cut off. I could thrash and kick—I fought off rape a time or two in the army before I got to Sgt. Rae's squad, where you'd better believe no

woman ever had to fear attack by fellow soldiers—but now I'm
sinking into sub space, wide open, vulnerable.

"What's got into you, Specialist? What do you think you
want?"

She knows, of course. By now we know almost everything
about each other. My face is level with hers, a rare treat, and I
try to focus on her face through my fog of obsession. The hair
that was mostly dark two years ago is more salt than pepper
now, and brush-cut shorter. There are lines around her eyes
from more than the desert sun. The squareness of her face, so
like her father's, is softened just enough by the graceful curve of
her cheeks that I want to stroke it with my fingers and then my
tongue, if I could only earn that privilege.

Sgt. Rae shifts so that her weight is mostly on the crossbar
and slides one hand free of its ring. "Speak up, Brown!" She
grabs my brown ponytail, yanks me close, and then shoves me
away so that I spin one way and then the other as the ropes
twist, untwist, and twist again. When I sway close enough she
swats me across my ass, or as close as she can reach, and I feel
it all the way down my butt cheeks and between my thighs. She
does it again, and then again, until the heat flows so deep inside
me I think I might explode.

With all her weight on the crossbar through her chest and
armpits, she reaches out to grip me by the shoulders, hard,
hurting me just the way I like it. Then her big hands slide under
my armpits so she's partly holding me up. My upstretched arms
raise my small breasts; she rubs her thumbs across my nipples so
hard and fast they must be standing out like bullets, and when
she pinches them, sharp pangs of pleasure shoot down through
my belly.

She knows where the worst of my scars are and works around
them down my sides and ribs, trying not to be too rough even

when I squirm and squeal and try to get even harder pressure from her fingers. I'm not silent any longer. It doesn't matter how I sound, what's pain and what's pleasure; all that matters is getting more and more.

Sgt. Rae's the one who has to use her safeword first. "At ease, Brown!" She grips the rings again and sinks slowly back into her chair.

My feet touch the ground. My arms drop, and I loosen the rope loops with my teeth, getting free just in time for her next order.

"Get over here, Jenny, stat!"

So I leap to straddle her lap, and she lifts me tight against her shoulder, right where I belong. Her free hand kneads my butt hard enough to make my cunt grind into her. I could come from that alone but she needs more, more of my skin and heat and wetness, so she gets my pants down and sighs approval when I'm slippery enough for her calloused fingers to move easily between my folds. Back and forth, teasing, pressing deeper, a knuckle nudging my clit on each forward stroke; I want it all now, now! But I have to wait for her to drive me even harder, higher. This isn't just for me.

"Now." Rae's voice is strained. "Feel it. For both of us." I'm rocking with her thrusts, howling with need, taking everything she can fit inside me, and when the pleasure bursts through all control, I shout my joy to the treetops loud enough for two hearts, two bodies.

She holds me tight while my breathing slows toward normal. When I raise my head I see a tear trickling down her cheek. This doesn't scare me the way it used to; I've figured out that it's her own release of tension after she's made me feel what she can't feel any more except through me. Being strong when that's what I need makes it safe to be vulnerable afterward.

Besides, now's my chance to lick the tear away, kiss my way all across the face I love, ending with the lips that say more this way than words ever could.

Rae sets me gently away sooner, though, than usual. "Jenny, there's something... Well, something that needs saying."

Now I'm scared. Hasn't everything already been said?

"You gave me back my life," she says, and pauses to search for the right words. "And I know you think I saved yours. So you could say there's no owing anything on either side."

I couldn't say that at all, so I just look at her. She sees my expression and strokes my face with such tenderness that fear melts away.

"I didn't mean... It's just that whatever we do, it's by choice. Maggie Burnside stopped by my desk today and asked, out of the blue, when we were going to get around to making things legal."

"Maggie the town clerk? Old Maggie Graniteside?"

"She's not so bad when you get to know her. And I guess she's come around to thinking we're not so bad, either. Or maybe she's decided to catch up with the twenty-first century without being dragged there."

"So what did you tell her?" I snuggle back against her side.

"I said the piece of paper might be nice to have, but it couldn't make us any closer, so I'd just go home and ask my wife."

"We might as well humor her, then. Set a good example."

There'll be more to say later, and plenty of time to say it. Now, with the afterglow of lovemaking intensified by the hum of the motor, we don't need words at all as the chair I built carries Sgt. Rae, and Sgt. Rae carries me home.

DEAD ON
HER FEET

Elizabeth L. Brooks

J amie kept her eyes closed, even though the plane was descending and she couldn't sleep. Nonessential travel, like finally coming home after two years in the godforsaken desert, was slow. And frustrating. She'd caught a supply truck from her unit's camp that ran three hours into the city base, and then waited around for most of a day for a military transport plane that had room for her, which had flown eight hours to Germany. Then it was a bus to take her to the commercial airport in Munich, where not a single ticketing agent could be found who spoke English. She'd made do, though—a soldier made do, even in some crazy backwater where a shovel-dug latrine was a luxury and female soldiers couldn't leave base without escort and even the kids you were there to help hated you for the uniform on your back.

But this was Germany, which was friendly and civilized and where the only thing in the way was words. That was easy, even allowing for her being tired and discombobulated from travel already. She'd pulled out her BlackBerry and loaded up an atlas and pointed and zoomed and pointed and zoomed until she'd finally made the crisply-dressed, ultra-polite young man under-stand her destination. Then it was commercial transport all the way, with its much more comfortable seats but its annoying security protocols (didn't they understand how goddamn hard it was to get in and out of combat boots?) and its annoyed civil-ians. Munich to London, London to New York, in and out of customs and security, retrieving and then rechecking her duffel every time she went through customs in a new country...

Thirty-four hours on the move and counting, dead on her feet, but this was the last flight and her ears were popping with the descent. Maybe another hour now and then she'd step out of the Atlanta airport into the lush, thick humidity of proper Southern air, maybe even one of those summertime afternoon deluges and she would stand there and just let the rain soak her right to the skin. Then she'd take a bus a couple of hours down into Georgia, to a tiny little town that no one had ever heard of who hadn't been born there, and then it was only a couple of miles from the bus depot to Casey's mama's house. To Casey.

Eyes still closed, Jamie's hand stole up to her shirt pocket where she kept the most important things: her passport, the receipts for all those planes and buses, her ID cards, the cash she'd drawn to pay for food...and the picture of her and Casey at his sister's wedding two years back. She'd looked ridiculous in that bridesmaid's dress with her fresh-from-basic close-cropped hair and those mannish muscles on her bare shoulders, but Casey had looked so very, very fine in that tux, and he'd pulled her close while they danced and told her she was the most beautiful woman there, and they'd snuck off down to the basement and almost not made it back in time to see the cake cut. Luckily the tux jacket had covered where she'd got lipstick on his cummerbund.

She didn't take the picture out, not here on the plane where everyone around her would be able to see her face, but she didn't need to. She'd looked at it so many times back in her sweltering bunk back at camp that she had it memorized. It was the image she called up in her mind's eye when she was trying to ignore hostile allies and murderous opponents, drinking two gallons of water a day just to keep her sweat glands from going into revolt, her teeth crunching on the nasty gray dust as she got into it *yet again* with those clowns from HQ who couldn't comprehend why shit kept breaking and she began to wonder if "back home" had ever even existed or if it had all been some kind of elaborate mirage or heatstroke hallucination.

Sometimes she was pretty sure it *had* been a hallucination, because men like Casey just didn't exist, not like she remembered him: tall and strong, drop-dead sexy when that mischievous twinkle shone in his pretty brown eyes; a good man who took care of his mama and adored his little nephew but wasn't averse to a little hell-raising to liven up a Friday night; a man who knew her better than she even knew herself sometimes. They'd grown up together; Jamie's mama and Casey's had been friends from the cradle, just like Jamie and Casey themselves, right up until they were fourteen and Casey had kissed her in the church basement while they were supposed to be counting up the pies for the mission bake sale. But he hadn't protested three years later when she'd told him she was going to enlist, hadn't tried to turn it into something about him or taken it as any kind of slight on his manhood or his ego. He'd told her he would miss her and told her he would write, and he'd promised to be waiting for her when she came home again.

And that part was the craziest of all, that he loved her—*her,* knob-kneed and flat-chested as she'd been all the way through adolescence, and he'd never so much as looked at another girl, not that she'd ever seen or even heard about, and even though she'd up and enlisted for five years, and still had two left to serve, he was waiting on her.

And that was where Angie down in motor pool always laughed and called bullshit on her. Most of the time, Jamie figured that was just jealousy, but sometimes she wondered. Angie'd taken Jamie under her wing when she'd arrived and she'd been right about all kinds of stuff that Jamie would've sworn was pure nonsense before she'd seen it play out just the way Angie'd said it would. And when Jamie had arrived with her unit fresh from the states, there'd been eight of them with girls back home (or guys, Jamie thought, since she was including herself in that, and Joe hadn't exactly been subtle, even before DADT had been repealed) and now, after two years, they were down to two of them. This long-distance stuff was *hard*.

But the plane was touching down now, and soon they'd be getting off and hiking through the terminal to the baggage claim and collecting her duffel full of dirty clothes and presents and then catching the shuttle over to the bus station for two weeks of leave before she had to report to her new post stateside. *Casey,* she thought, *I'm almost home.* Just a couple more hours.

Duffel. Shuttle. Bus. The list of steps that had been so long when she'd started her leave was now down to just these three short items. She repeated them to herself like a litany as she joined the flow of passengers streaming off the plane. *Duffel. Shuttle. Bus.*

Everything here was in English, but Jamie was so tired that the words on the signs were blurring. She had to ask the gate attendant which way to go even though she'd been through Atlanta a dozen times or more. She got on the tram that would take her to baggage claim. There were seats available, but Jamie knew if she sat down she'd fall asleep. She waved forward a short, plump woman shepherding two small children. The woman smiled gratefully and thanked her before lifting the little boy up into a seat beside his sister. Jamie leaned against a wall and closed her eyes. Maybe she'd be able to nap on the bus a little. It'd be a shame to waste any of her precious leave at home with something as mundane as sleep.

Duffel. Shuttle. Bus. The tram lurched to its final stop, and Jamie stumbled off with the rest of the crowd. There was a large board there that would tell her where to go for her bag, but it had white text on a blue background that was all but impossible for Jamie's exhaustion-fogged eyes to read. Dead on her feet, she squinted to make the words readable and tried blearily to recall what her flight number had been.

"Jamie Kaye!"

The airport disappeared around her, fading into utter insignificance as she whipped around in shock. He'd put on a little weight, but it looked good on him—he'd always been so skinny his mama had threatened to hire him out as a scarecrow. He'd let his hair grow out a little, too; it wasn't long, but it wasn't the buzz cut he'd maintained since the eighth grade, either. That would take some getting used to. His eyes were the same, though, the exact same dark golden brown as the filling in his mama's homemade pecan pie, and just as sweet, crinkled with his smile.

"Casey," she whispered, and then she shrieked, "Casey!" and flung herself into his arms.

"What the hell are you doing here?" she demanded, and then kissed him so he couldn't answer; it was a stupid question, she didn't care about the answer, she just wanted him to kiss her until they'd made up for six months of letters and whispered phone calls and for-fuck's-sake awkward video chats in the base's computer lab.

And he did. He kissed her like she was the last drop of water in the desert, the first taste of a decadent dessert, like she was the only thing in the world that mattered. His hands were in her hair, on her shoulders, pulling her hips into his, everywhere. When they broke apart because they had to breathe, he nuzzled at her neck, his breath sighing down to tickle her collarbone. "Goddamn, you smell good, Jamie Kaye," he groaned.

Jamie laughed hoarsely. She hadn't showered in two days, hadn't changed her fatigues or put on deodorant in nearly as long. She was amazed he could stand to be so close to her, frankly. She pulled away to look at him again, still not certain she wasn't dreaming. "Casey," she started to say, and then she registered the way he was dressed.

He was in a tuxedo, all black, with a blackberry-colored tie and cummerbund. His wavy, honey-colored hair had been slicked back into something resembling neatness and a spray of flowers decorated his lapel. Jamie blinked at him again.

"Casey," she said again, her mind reeling, "what the hell is this?"

He glanced down at himself, self-conscious grin briefly teasing his lips. "Well," he drawled sheepishly, "when you sent me that text message when you got to New York with your flight info to Atlanta, I...kind of had me a notion."

"A notion?" Jamie asked skeptically.

Casey was not often the kind of man who had notions. Far more often, it was his dumbass cousins who had the notions, and then a week or two later, when the bail had been paid or the insurance had been settled up, Casey would send her a letter and tell her all about it. She crossed her arms over her chest and waited expectantly.

Casey knew exactly what she was thinking, she could tell by the sudden uncertainty in his eyes. "See," he plunged onward, "I've been thinking... You remember my sister's wedding, I expect—"

Jamie did not—did *not*—touch her shirt pocket with that picture in it, but she could feel her face begin to heat. "I remember," she allowed.

Casey grinned at her again and her blood heated, her nipples and cunt tingling like they always had when he'd flashed that grin her way, though she was damned if she'd let him know it right now, standing here in the middle of the goddamn Atlanta airport.

"I'd been meaning to ask that night," he said. "After Sue and Darryl were safely away, I mean. But then you told me about your posting, and...it didn't seem quite the right time, anymore."

Jamie was frowning. "The right time for what?"

Casey shrugged, a ripple of wiry shoulders. "But now I think maybe I just chickened out. I've been thinking about it so much these last few weeks. I know you've still got a couple of years left before you have to decide if you're going to re-up, but the thought just wouldn't leave me, and when I knew you were just a few hours from home, I decided I couldn't wait even an hour longer than I had to."

Casey knelt down right there in the airport. People were watching, most of them looking amused. "Jamie Kaye Carmine," he intoned solemnly, though his dark eyes sparkled, "I've loved you for all my life, and I intend to love you for every bit of the rest of it, too. Would you do me the honor—"

Jamie's face was flaming. "Damn it, Casey, get up off the floor and stop making a spectacle!"

"—of consenting to be my bride, to have and to—"

"Yes!" She laughed, yanking at his arm. "Yes, you idiot, of course I will, but get *up!*"

Casey surged upward and pulled her back into his arms and she didn't resist, even though their audience was laughing and applauding. His mouth tasted of peaches and whiskey and breath mint, and it was the taste of home. She melted into the embrace, holding him tighter, letting him hold her up since she was so damned tired. Rumpled and filthy with the detritus and sweat of what seemed like dozens of airports and bus stations— and he still wanted her; she could feel his arousal even through the clothes that separated them.

Jamie plunged into the kiss, giving him every lonely and frightened night halfway around the world when she'd wished for him to hold her, every furtive and half-frantic scramble for relief while her bunkmate was in the head, every desperate kiss she'd used to seal her letters.

It was Casey who broke this time, panting hard as he leaned his forehead against hers. "God," he muttered, "I don't know if I can stand to wait till we get home."

A soldier makes do. Jamie looked around quickly, not quite daring to hope, but—there were four soldiers coming out of the men's restroom, huge duffels over their shoulders. She grabbed Casey's hand and dragged him along in her wake.

They halted at her approach. Automatic as breathing, Jamie checked their insignia. "Sergeant," she offered in greeting to their leader.

"Private," he returned. He glanced at Casey and then back to her, and his mouth curved. "Just getting home, Private?"

"Haven't even got my bag out of claim yet," she said.

"Baggage claim takes forever," opined one of the other men, another private.

"Yeah," said a third. "And there's always a line for the damn

head." He glanced around quickly for patrolling airport security, then gave a quick head jerk toward the restroom door.

Jamie grinned. "Thanks, guys." She would have dragged
Casey into the bathroom with her, except that he was already
pushing her forward.

There was no lock on the door, but Jamie didn't care. She
leaned against the wall between two urinals, already yanking
her shirt loose, pulling it over her head without bothering to
unbutton it.

"Those guys won't prank us, will they?" Casey asked, lips
already at her throat, his hands fumbling behind her for the
hooks on her bra. "They'll keep everyone out?"

Jamie yanked her hands free of her shirt cuffs and dropped
it to the floor. "Dunno," she admitted.

Her own unit wouldn't do that to her—but they might do it to
someone else that they didn't know. "Doesn't matter, really."

She yanked at the cummerbund, pushing it up and out of the
way so she could get to the fly of his pants. She couldn't help but
giggle at the memory of his sister's wedding, but it turned into a
gasp as Casey's mouth closed on her breast.

After six months of nothing but her own hands and memories, it was electrifying to feel his tongue on her nipple, sliding
and flicking, hot and wet. Casey moaned and his hips thrust,
his hardness unmistakable. She resumed working her way into
his pants.

When her hand closed on his cock, he grunted and thrust
again, and she squeezed gently. "God, you feel good," she
groaned.

His hand was inside her pants now, and she was already
wet, had been since he'd gone down on his knees in front of
her. Jamie tried to lift a leg and give him greater access, but
her pants were trapped by her boots—why the fuck hadn't she

changed into civvies back in New York?

"Dammit!" she cursed, struggling with the fabric.

"Shh," Casey soothed. Two steps put them in front of the bank of sinks, facing the mirrors. Casey stood behind her, his hands on her breasts, stroking and circling. Jamie watched, fascinated, as his fingers plucked at her nipples, pinching and then soothing, until she was trembling with need. He pushed gently then and she leaned over, bracing her arms on the countertop and opening her legs as wide as the binding pants would allow. Casey's eyes met hers in the mirror as he pressed in close.

It was even more awkward than at his sister's wedding—at least she'd been wearing a dress then—but they were both needing each other so damned bad right now. Jamie couldn't open her legs any wider, but she managed to lean onto her arms until her toes barely touched the floor, lifting her hips higher. Grateful for every damned push-up the fucking drill sergeant had put her through, she twisted and contorted until—*ohfuckinghellfinally*—his cock was in her, hot and heavy.

Each thrust made the whole countertop quiver; the vibrations in the mirror bank leached some of the heat from his reflected gaze. Jamie felt a hysterical giggle threaten to rise but it felt good, better than good, nearly perfect, and the laughter died in her throat to be reborn as a moan. Casey's hand slipped between her legs and he growled possessively when his fingers slid between her folds. His rough calluses were the perfect friction against her swollen clit, and Jamie had to bite her lip to keep from screaming with pleasure.

"Oh, God, Jamie Kaye," he groaned, "you feel so good, so damn good..." His movements were growing jerkier, rougher. "God, Jamie," Casey panted. His voice was carried away as he came, and Jamie could feel him spurting, the pulsing spasms of his cock stretching her in the best possible way.

He froze for a moment, catching his breath, and then redou-
bled his efforts between her legs. His fingers dragged and teased
and tugged, pitting their roughness against the slick wetness of
her need, his cock still inside her, softening but still big enough
for her to squeeze with each tremor of her body. She became
aware that she was whimpering but her voice was no longer
under her control.

The orgasm started in her toes and rushed upward like a
desert sunrise, hot and crackling, leaving her body trembling
and weak in its wake. Casey held her upright and gently stroked
her skin until she could stand again, then turned her to kiss
her.

"Come on, Jamie Kaye," he whispered as he helped her clean
up and get her clothes back on. "I can see you're dead on your
feet. Let's get you home where I can take care of you properly."

Jamie smiled up at Casey, kissed him gently. "Where we can
take care of each other," she corrected. "As it should be."

OUT OF TIME

J.K. Coi

It had taken David almost an hour to charm the address of this modest apartment building from the army nurses at the base. Steve hadn't understood why he needed so desperately to come here instead of to the airstrip to see him off.

His little brother had just finished three months of extended training overseas—during which time he'd been pretty much unreachable—and although he'd only arrived back home yesterday, he was shipping out again in the very early morning.

He couldn't explain to Steve that the thought of watching him get on the plane only made him feel worse about everything he'd recently lost, so he'd taken him aside and told him good-bye at the hospital.

"Be careful, little brother." He'd given him a tight bear hug even though his still-healing wounds ached in protest.

"Keep a light on, eh?" Steve grinned. The saying had been one of their father's, who'd been an officer for thirty years before rejoining civilian life and finally settling down with his family—only to be killed in a car accident, along with his wife, when the boys were still teens. David had done all he could from then on to take care of his brother.

Steve had just received confirmation of his first permanent assignment. David tried not to let his recent experiences affect the younger man's enthusiasm. After all, he loved the army too. It had been his life for nine years, and if not for the injury that got him shipped back home, he'd still be doing what he could to protect the country he loved.

It was one thing to give himself to the cause, but David's sudden brush with mortality had unsettled him. He was afraid for his little brother on his way to Afghanistan.

Making his way slowly up the short concrete steps, he shifted the hated cane to his other hand to open the front door before entering the tiny lobby. The second set of doors leading inside didn't open when he yanked on the handle. He saw the buzzer next to a square microphone and glanced left at the row of mailboxes on the wall, looking for Katie's name.

Could she really have put him out of her mind already—the patient in bed 114 with a shattered kneecap and no family or friends to visit him for most of his hospital stay? Maybe she'd only been doing her job, and now that he was no longer part of that job....

But David couldn't forget her, and when she hadn't come to see him before he was released, he knew he had to try to find out why.

Ah, there she was. He tapped the mailbox that displayed her name. *O'Meara, Apt. 302.* Contrary to a few of the other boxes, the printing on the label was crisp and black as if it had just been posted.

He pressed the call button and waited.

"Yes?"

Even through the fuzziness of the intercom, he recognized her voice. It was the same husky voice that had gotten him through five weeks in a hospital bed. The same voice he'd started hearing in his dreams. Hot, sexy dreams that caused him to wake with a hard on like he hadn't had since he was a teenager, and no way to relieve the pressure because of the nurses and doctors constantly in and out of his room.

"Katie, it's me. David." He bent forward to speak into the microphone and waited for her response.

She didn't answer.

He pushed the button again.

"I'm still here, David." She didn't sound as happy to hear his voice as he was to hear hers.

He took a deep breath, bending just a little more to rub his aching knee. Maybe this had been a mistake. If she'd really felt something for him, she would have met him at the hospital.

Could he really have read her so wrong? Misinterpreted this thing between them so badly?

"Katie, please. Can I see you?"

He looked up. On the other side of the double doors, a woman dressed in a bright purple velour tracksuit was exiting the elevator carrying a tiny dog under one arm. A bright purple leash dangled from her other hand. He watched her approach even as he listened to Katie's heavy sigh through the intercom.

"I don't know if that's such a good idea," she said.

"The door's opening, Katie. I'm coming up." He gave her the courtesy of a warning, but even if she protested, he didn't think he could give up the opportunity to get inside, not when it meant seeing her at least one more time.

Thankfully, she didn't respond and he slipped past the stranger, who eyed his cane as she exited the building while her little dog leaned forward in her arms to try to sniff him.

Before his injury he would have taken the stairs, and he was just stubborn enough to try it now, but he didn't want to get to Katie's door three hours later huffing and puffing like an old man, so he pushed the button for the elevator. On the third floor, he counted suite numbers until he faced the door at the end of the hall.

302.

Before he could knock, it swung open, leaving his fist hanging in midair. He dropped it, taking in his first sight of Katie dressed in civilian clothing with her long hair hanging down around her shoulders instead of pulled back in a tight bun.

He was used to seeing her dressed professionally, in scrubs or fatigues. That had been a turn-on in and of itself. In fact, David had fucked his fair share of female soldiers over the years for just that reason. But right now he couldn't remember what the draw of a uniform had been because jeans and a T-shirt seemed the most erotic use for cotton ever invented.

The dark blue denim rode low and hugged her hips, while the light pink T-shirt was snug and came up short at the midriff so her little belly button peeked beneath it. The material pulled taut across her full breasts, drawing attention to her pert nipples…and dear fucking lord she wasn't wearing a bra.

It was impossible not to stare, but he slowly brought his gaze back up. She lifted her arm and braced it against the edge of the open door, hip kicked out in a pose that dragged the edge of her shirt up a little higher.

"What are you doing here, David?"

How to tell her he had to see her and not sound like a stalker? "I was released from the hospital today."

She finally smiled and nodded. "I can see that."

"I needed to see you."

With a deep breath, she dropped her arm and stepped to

the side. She pursed her lips and he thought she was going to tell him to take a hike, but finally she blew out a long breath and said, "All right. You might as well come on in for a few minutes."

Even though he was technically getting what he wanted—the opportunity to see her again—his chances for anything more than that didn't sound promising. He walked inside, trying like hell not to use the damn cane.

He waited in the entrance until she'd closed and locked the door behind him. When she came around and moved farther into the apartment, he followed.

He frowned. She had no furniture. About four or five boxes were stacked against the walls, all neatly labeled. KITCHEN. BEDROOM. BOOKS. He remembered the nameplate on her mailbox. "Did you just move in?"

"I've been here about six months." She walked into the kitchen, where a jug of water sat on the counter next to a glass with ice in it. Pouring the water, she looked up at him with a raised brow. "Would you like some?"

He nodded and leaned his cane up against the wall. "Thanks. I guess you haven't had much time for unpacking?"

With a shrug, she turned and reached to open a cupboard. He was entranced with the way her short T-shirt slipped up her torso again. God, he wanted to crowd up behind her, slide his hands underneath that shirt, push it over her tits and squeeze her nipples tight while he bent her over the counter....

"I did unpack," she finally admitted, "but I just boxed everything back up again." As she pulled out another glass he noticed that the only other thing in the cupboard was a single plate. He cleared his throat when she turned back around and poured the water. She handed him the glass.

"Why?" He knew the answer to that. He didn't want to

know, but now it was all too obvious. She was shipping out.

She lifted deep brown eyes to his and sighed. "I'm on a flight tonight, David."

He clenched his hand around the cool glass. "Afghanistan?"

She nodded.

"Why didn't you tell me?"

She put her glass back down on the counter and met his gaze. There was resignation there, as if she'd done this same song and dance before. "Why do you care?"

"How can you ask me that?" Stepping forward, he reached for her hand. "If it weren't for you, I wouldn't have made it through the last few weeks. You saved my life in that hospital."

She put her hand on his chest to stop him from getting too close, but chuckled too, maybe to make the action seem less than what it was—a rejection. "I did no such thing, Captain."

He didn't know what she meant to accomplish by using his designation, unless it was a further attempt to force some formality between them. "I changed some bedding and read to you so that you wouldn't go Incredible Hulk on us and tear the place apart from boredom. I would have done it for any patient, and I'd hardly call it lifesaving medicine."

Did she spend hours with every patient, talking about past and future, hopes and dreams? Did she read to every patient tirelessly when they said they liked the sound of her voice? And did she *kiss* all her patients or let them pull her into bed with them?

"It was more than that, and you know it."

Her gaze dropped, but he saw the flush in her cheeks and was encouraged, just a little.

He let himself remember too. For the first few weeks, she'd been his only distraction from the pain and boredom. Steve hadn't shown up until the day before he was due to be released. Waiting for her in between rehab and bandage changes had been torture, but then every once in a while he'd look up and find her standing in the doorway smiling at him.

It was like sunshine and music, making his heart beat faster and bringing a lightness to his soul that he'd never felt before.

The last time she visited him she'd been off duty. He thought she looked tired and cajoled her until she climbed into the bed beside him. He'd put his arm around her while they talked. It got late and they both fell asleep. When he awoke, her face had been pressed into the hollow of his throat, and she'd thrown a leg over his thighs. His arm cradled her close, hand curved over her ribs just beneath the tempting swell of her breast.

He remembered the way she'd felt in his arms. The warmth of her, the subtle scent of her floral perfume, and the silky softness of her hair tickling his chin. He'd started to think that being stuck in that bed was the best thing that had ever happened to him.

Nothing had ever felt so good or so natural as talking to Katie, laughing with Katie, waking up next to Katie...until the moment their lips had met in a fusion of the desire and heat that had been building between them as they'd spent more and more time together.

Then natural had taken on a whole new meaning.

He'd tangled his hand in her hair and she'd let out a sexy little groan and melted into him.

The kiss had quickly gotten out of hand, neither one of them noticing or caring that one of the nurses was probably due to check on him soon. He'd devoured her mouth with lips and teeth until she opened for him and took his stabbing tongue. Her hand slipped down to test the length of his hard cock under the bed sheets and then he'd been the one groaning as he thrust with hard jerks into her palm.

The more he got to know the woman, the more he wanted to

find a way to keep seeing her.

Yes, she was a soldier, volunteering at the base hospital while on leave because she needed the hours, but he supposed she'd be heading out again sometime soon. It hadn't mattered to him then and it didn't matter now. All that mattered was holding on to this connection in whatever way he could.

"Katie, what time do you have to leave?" he asked now, clearing his throat. "How long do we have?"

His body ached for her, but all he really wanted to do was memorize her face, her voice, and then he could leave if he had to, with the scent of her on his skin as a parting gift.

A stricken look creased her brow. "This is why I stayed away from the hospital today," she admitted. "I didn't want to be forced to say good-bye to you."

He took her by the shoulders. Her breath hitched at the contact but she didn't pull away. "Why? It doesn't have to be good-bye forever. I'll be here. I'll be waiting."

She barked out a hoarse chuckle. "How can you say that? We've only known each other a few weeks, and you were relegated to a hospital bed. You had no other choice but to put up with me."

"Do you really believe that?" He shook her gently. "All those days and hours we spent together may not have been my idea of the perfect first dates, but we got to know each other pretty well, don't you think?"

He didn't know her as well as he'd thought, though, or he'd know why she was running scared now.

"You know about my crappy youth and how much I despise green Jell-O. I told you about my parents and that I still feel responsible for my little brother."

She nodded.

He looked into her eyes. "And you know my fear that I'll

never amount to anything now that my military career has been shot to hell." He glanced down at his leg. "Literally."

"But, David—"

"No buts," he interrupted. "I know you too."

A brow cocked and her chin went up. "You think because I told you some stuff, that you know me?"

She was getting defensive now. He took that as a sign she was cracking and pushed harder. "I think I know why you're trying so hard to deny what's between us. It's happened before, hasn't it? What? Did he screw around while you were deployed? Did he promise he'd be waiting and then fall in love with someone else?"

Her glare made him wince inwardly, but he dared not show her. He dared not back down or he'd lose this last chance with her.

Finally, she sighed. "He died. I was overseas and he was hit head-on by a fucking truck."

"Ah, Jesus." He felt like an ass and pulled her close, cradling her head to his chest. "Baby, I'm sorry."

"I don't want to go through that again, David."

"I understand, Katie. But you can't avoid loss or heartache forever. You'll only cheat yourself out of the chance to find something really great. Something that would be worth the risk." He grinned and ran his hands up and down her arms. "That would be me, in case you were wondering. So, if that's all you've got by way of excuses, then I'm stripping off your clothes right now."

"You think so?"

"If you're on the red-eye tonight, I still have a couple hours to make sure you'll be counting every day until you can come back to me."

Her eyes widened, but a smile curved her lips. "You're really that good?"

"Only one way to find out, isn't there?"

She eyed his leg. "I don't have a bed anymore. It went into storage this afternoon."

"I can work without it as long as we don't get too acrobatic." He shrugged, hoping that would be the truth. "But I promise, when you return I'll have built my strength back up so that I can take you wherever and however you desire."

"Oh yeah?" Her arms crossed in front of her, hands gripping the hem of her T-shirt, but she paused before lifting it. "I'll have time to think of something really good, so you'd better be prepared."

She dragged the shirt slowly up her body. He groaned when her perfect, naked breasts came into view, and then she pulled the garment all the way over her head and dropped it to the floor.

"Baby," he drawled, "with you, it's always going to be good."

He watched her as she closed the short distance between them and all he could think about was how desperate she made him feel, how he wanted her screaming his name.

She stretched onto her toes and wrapped her arms around his neck. "And what if I want you to fuck me right here? And again up against the wall over there? What if I want to do it doggie-style on the carpet in front of the window, and then push you onto your back and ride you until the very moment I have to leave?"

God, he really hoped he could do all that.

His hands splayed over the small of her back and slid upward. He twisted her long hair around his fist and tugged until her head fell back, giving him unrestricted access to her throat. "We had better get started, then."

He continued to whisper in her ear, torturing her with words between scorching kisses up and down her neck. "Do you have any idea how amazing you are? That I can't wait to feel you come apart in my arms?"

Her breathing hitched. "Oh yes, David. That's what I want."

Finally, he spun her around so that she faced the counter and cabinets. Pressing his chest to her back, he dropped a kiss to her shoulder, then pushed her hair out of the way and dragged his mouth up the column of her neck until she shivered.

He took his time fondling her breasts, pinching and pulling at her nipples until they stood up in rock-hard points. She started to work the buckle of her belt, but he pushed her hands away and did it himself, shoving the denim down her legs, which were sculpted and muscled from a career in the military.

"God, you're gorgeous." He dropped kisses down her spine until he could bend no more. His leg injury twinged as he straightened, but the slight pain only added another layer to his blissful torment.

When she stepped out of her jeans and the only thing left was her tiny pink thong, he knew he was done for. He pulled her close and pressed his denim-clad thighs to her ass, cupping her breast with one hand and snaking the other beneath the silky material over her mound.

Two fingers slipped inside her nice and easy. He pushed deep and her pussy clenched. "Oh fuck, that's good." She was so wet, coating his fingers with slippery cream as he worked her harder.

"David," she whimpered, letting her head fall back against his shoulder.

Her mouth opened and her eyes closed. He loved watching her. "Come for me, Katie."

She turned her face toward him and he cupped her chin for a kiss, the fingers of his other hand moving in her, thumb circling her clit until she moaned and started shuddering in his arms.

"Ahh, more." She tensed and arched, her ass pressing back into the cradle of his hips. "Fuck me, please."

He fumbled his pants open, pulled a condom from his pocket—yes, he'd been optimistic—and tore it open. He rolled it on and pushed her forward with a hand on her neck. Arms spread wide, she held on to the edge of the countertop. He probed the entrance of her pussy with the tip of his sheathed cock.

"Do it," she urged, tilting her ass higher. "Oh god, do it hard. Do it now—"

She gasped as he thrust into her, sliding right to the hilt in one forceful move that pushed her knees into the cupboards.

Heaven.

Oh yeah. She was tight and warm and perfect. He tried to hold still and savor the culmination of weeks of wanting her, but she was already sliding forward and back on him and the sight of his cock disappearing between the cheeks of her round ass was too much. Soon her restless little attempts to make him start moving threw him over the edge.

"Think of this while you're gone." His voice was gruff and hoarse, his throat tight. He fucked her with long, deep strokes, loving the way the tension built higher and higher with each one. "Think of me and how much I'll be missing you."

She whimpered, her body shaking just before the wild spasms of her pussy started squeezing him and he couldn't hold back any longer. He wrapped his arm around her waist and thrust one last time before giving in to the release.

When she turned in his arms, he gathered her close and buried his face in her hair, still breathing heavily. The sweat on their skin started to dry and stick them together, and his leg ached, but he didn't care.

"Oh, David," she whispered. "I'm going to miss you. I knew I was in trouble the first day I saw you. Why did we have to meet now when we can't have any time together?"

His arms tightened. "We have tonight. And that'll have to be enough to get me to your next leave."

She stroked his chest and sighed. "What will you do while I'm gone?"

"I'll find a way to put my life back together. Find something I can do here with a gimp leg and a former military background." He'd already gotten a few calls for positions that would mean he could stay in the service, so he wasn't feeling as pessimistic about his options as he had only days ago.

He gazed into her eyes. "And I'll be waiting."

It wouldn't be what he'd planned...but he hadn't planned on Katie O'Meara either. Yet here they were and he'd never been happier, despite the fact that she would be leaving in just a few short hours.

She smiled up at him. "Then keep a light on for me."

DONE

Charlotte Stein

He always comes to me this way. Skin smelling of something I can't identify and probably shouldn't want to, fresh new scars littering his body, that look in his eyes like I don't know what. Sometimes it's as though someone has punched both of them out, even though there are no bruises around that hollow gaze. And sometimes it's like a fire is in there, burning down the house of him.

But mostly I just can't tell, because he's Jack and he does things for his country and what does it really matter anyway? Jack isn't even his real name. It's probably something less clipped and generically exciting, like Peter or Paul. Or even something ridiculous, like Dwayne or Dwight.

Though I make do with Jack because without it he'd just be the man with no name who comes to my house and does unspeakable things to me for one day out of every sixty. I'd be a whole new version of the Fugitive, only my bad guy is missing a moniker instead of an arm, and rather than killing my spouse he just fucks me up against a whole variety of things until I come, and come, and come.

I figure my version is unlikely to star Harrison Ford—I can't imagine Harrison Ford speaking some of the dialogue from my particular movie. Like in the bar that first time, when he'd told me he just wanted to get his face between my legs. That he wanted to spread me over something and lick my little clit until I screamed.

Yeah, I can't imagine many people saying something like that.

But he does, because he's straight to the point. He's direct in a way other people never get to be, with all of their hours and hours of time to go on dates and negotiate sex and make everything nice with hearts and flowers.

Instead, he comes in my door like a gunshot and tells me right off: *I've been thinking of that pussy, baby. I've been thinking of it so hard and long I forget my own name.*

So I suppose that's why he's just Jack. Because my cunt hypnotized him and made him lose it someplace I can't even imagine. And though I know that's a ridiculous thing to think, it stays with me when he gets up from the table. It matches the sight of his cock, all thick and stiff beneath the material of his rough pants.

Could be he does think about me that way, if he's hard before we've finished the dinner I made. Before he's finished his drink—a beer he's barely touched, really—and such a sight to see. I don't mind admitting that my mouth goes dry, and that could be because he's hot.

He's big and roped with more muscle than I'm used to, eyes all dark like that hollow I always think of, the stubble on his shaved head so fine it's almost a grain. It's the insides of a strip of wood, and as smooth as that to the touch.

But it's not any of those things that speak to me. That make me wet before he's laid a finger on me, so ready to feel him fucking into my defenseless body.

It's his hunger. His complete greed for the feel of me, after so many months away doing god knows what. It's like he can hardly contain himself, like a hurricane in my house, just waiting to take everything apart.

And he does. He takes *me* apart. He pulls open the front of my dress without saying a word, hands so heavy and rough on me. And when I make a little sound—a little shocked note of protest, maybe—he kisses my suddenly bared breasts by way of apology.

"Fuckin' beautiful," he tells me, and it's the strangest thing. I've never felt the word had quite the same ring of truth as when he says it. Even with the swearing shunted right up against its ass, I feel it keenly, I feel it perfectly.

I am beautiful when he kisses my breasts and cups my backside in his big hands, all of him so voracious somehow it's impossible to resist.

And oh god, he's so *strong*. I won't deny that's anything but a bonus. Where other men would squeeze and be done with it, he uses that tight—near-painful—grip to lift me clean off my feet, my legs going around his waist like a reflex. That mouth now on my throat as he grinds me hard against that stiff length between his thighs.

And then he tells me. He tells me things that should be embarrassing, that would be embarrassing if someone else said them, but somehow aren't with him.

"Oh yeah," he tells me as he rubs right over my cotton-clad pussy, "I can almost feel how wet you are, baby. You want it, huh? You want my cock in your cunt."

I'd hate it if another man used that word. I'd shut him down, tell him off. But then again, another man wouldn't say it the way Jack does—like he's praying to a god I don't have.

"Please," I say, because that's how I feel right now. I'm one big *please,* one big long need for him inside me, and he doesn't disappoint. He gets me on the kitchen table, slides my panties down my legs. Exposes my pussy in a way I've never been exposed before—two fingers either side of my slit, spreading me open.

"Oh, look at that," he says, though I don't have to. I can imagine what it looks like just by the feel of it—all of the wetness easing between the cheeks of my ass, my clit just one big long thrum before he's even touched it.

And then he does touch it, and I sob for him. I writhe on the kitchen table, pinned more effectively than a bug.

"Mmm, yeah," he says, and then he does something that should make me blush tomorrow. It should, but I know it won't. Tomorrow I'll think of it and masturbate instead, because just the image of him spitting right over my little swollen bud will be enough to get me going.

It's such a dirty thing. It's so rude. And yet oh, it feels so good when he works that extra bit of slickness over and around my clit. He just does it with the pad of his thumb until I'm half-crazy, then works and works it until I'm all the way there. All the way into crazy and out the other side, crying and begging him to just fuck me.

"Give it to me," I tell him, but he waits. I don't know where he gets the patience from, with those things he said about forgetting his name still hanging between us, but somehow he finds it. He's like a worked rod of iron, molded into something steely and straight.

And then just when I'm sure I can't take it anymore, he starts stripping out of those clothes.

Of course, it's always a treat. Always. I even like some of the smallest, strangest things about him, like the weird tautness of his belly button, as though his muscles have forced it to nearly disappear. Or the way the sinew in his left shoulder is just a little bit off, because he's obviously hurt himself at some point but naturally won't tell me how.

He doesn't tell me about the scars, either, but that's okay. I kiss them all anyway, because when I do he shows me the only unrestrained reaction he has—a kind of guttural *oh,* just for me. All for me, my man with no name.

"Turn over, baby," he says, and I do. Though I wonder the same thing as always as I press my belly to the table. As I let my legs trail off it, almost but not quite touching the ground.

Is it because this is too much? Is it too much to look at my face when he fucks me?

I don't know, I don't know, but I *do* know that he asks me to turn over often enough to always think about it the second he says it. And then when I'm done thinking about him I think about me and how I would feel to have him over me. Those eyes of his like something burnt out but still on fire, staring into mine as he went about this thing we're doing.

Of course I know the answer. And it tells me why he does it, it always tells me the reason why: It would feel like heaven. It would feel like hell.

"Fuck me," I demand, and it's bad enough when his hands go to my hips. It's bad enough when he tells me to spread myself for him, and I do. It's bad enough when I feel him urging himself against my always tightly clenching cunt, and then finally, finally...

He slides in. So steady and slow, for someone with shaking hands.

And shaking thighs.

I can feel them against my own, just going and going, but that's not really what I'm thinking about. Instead, my mind goes to the peculiar, being-taken-apart sensation I always get, the second he fills me up.

And I understand, in that brief moment of bliss, what it means. I recognize it for what it is, for the first time: relief. I'm relieved that he's inside me again, taking me so slow and easy. In a second, he'll descend into that pounding, fierce, frantic kind of rhythm, and I'll come in about a second.

But for now there's just the sense of his body, his hands on me, his cock in my pussy. His voice, like something I'd wait longer than sixty days to hear. *I'd wait a hundred for you. I'd wait a thousand. I'd wait in years, not days, just to know that you're here again with me.*

And then I'm not sure what happens to me, because I reach my hand up to my face and only afterward realize I've done it so he won't know about the wet that's on my face. I've done it so that *I* won't know about the wet that's on my face.

It's too late for that, though—I understand. The wet is still on my fingers and that feeling is still in my throat, even though he's fucking me hard enough to get right up against that sweet little place inside me. The one that only blooms when he touches me, when he takes me, when he says my name in a way I wish I could say his.

"Hilly," he pants, and oh I wish, I wish, I wish I had a better name than that. I wish I was like him, with a new and secret identity. *Yvette,* I'd be, or maybe *Natassja,* with a *J.* And I'd visit him in some cold country in a room that's bare except for a lightbulb, and say something mysterious and deadly, like:

Your time is up, Jackson.

Because apparently in my head his name is Jack Jackson and everything is a bit like an episode of *Rocky and Bullwinkle.*

Whereas in reality, he's fucking me frantically, near viciously, as though maybe there's no tomorrow.

And most of the time, I'm sure there won't be. There won't be a tomorrow. Everything is in his gaze, in his hands on me, in the way he takes me like this until my body arches and I scrabble to hold something on him, anything on him.

"Yeah, that's it baby, give it up," he tells me, which sounds rough but isn't. It isn't, because the second he says it he clasps my frantically clawing hand. He works me slower, softer, sweeter, and then just waits for my orgasm to sing out of me like some kind of goddamn love song.

"Ohhhh, Jack," I say to him when it happens, and I swear to god there's something else behind my sigh. More words I want to say, but never do. I can't say them when he's fucking me, in the middle of my orgasm.

But who am I really fooling? I can't say them any other time, either. Instead I just let the pleasure surge through me, thick and forceful. I let my cunt clench hard around his still-working cock until he tells me, clearly: *oh there's nothing on earth like the feel of your sweet pussy.*

And that has to be enough.

Or at least, I think it has to be. I'm sure it has to be, right up to the point where he stops fucking me and gathers me up in his arms. Takes me to a place we almost never go, like my bedroom. Spreads me out on the sheets, with his arms still around me.

And then I'm not sure of anything, anymore. All I can do is hold on as he does the thing I always thought he wouldn't. He takes me on my back, with one big arm still around my shoulders and those eyes holding mine—not burnt out at all, not even on fire.

Like melting chocolate, I think they are, just before he kisses my mouth over and over. As he says to me *you're beautiful, you're beautiful, my lovely Hilly. My girl,* he says, so that I have to just hold tight and hide my face in his shoulder.

I am your girl, I think, *but I won't be soon.*

Soon he'll get up, and get dressed, and go away again. Everything will go back to how it was as though he barely even leaves a print on anything—though that's wrong, isn't it?

He leaves a print on me. He has pushed his thumb into the formless shape of me and left an indentation forever. I can still feel him, after he's gone. I can still smell his steely smell, still feel his hands on me, still hear him saying what he's saying now.

"Oh fuck, you're gonna make me come," he tells me, which I suppose sounds singularly unromantic, in the face of all the thoughts I've just been having. But here's the thing—it isn't. It can't be, because no other man lets me know things like that. No other man makes me feel the way he does, as though I'm worth something.

I give him something, and he's grateful for it.

He moans against the side of my face, and oh, that's even sweeter. It makes me clutch at him, pleasure swelling in me, again. Everything now so wet between my legs that I can hear it and he can feel it—and he tells me so. He tells me how slippery I am, how good it is, how much he wants to just let go, let go.

And when he does, it's glorious. It's like that heaven and hell I thought of, only a moment ago, because on the one hand I can see and feel every little part of him, all exposed—his pleasure-glazed eyes, the shudder that goes through him, the swell of his thick cock inside me.

But on the other, all of those things mean it's over. It's over. In a second, he'll stop looking at me like that—as though he isn't someplace faraway and too horrible to mention. And his arm will unwind from around my shoulder, and all of the delicious shaking he's doing will stop and I'll have to pretend again that I don't love him.

Only then he asks, "Is it okay if I stay?"

Without a single hint that he's going to do it. There's nothing that suggests it in the way he eventually rolls off me—even though that arm stays around my shoulders. Even though I can feel a shift, just creeping in around the edges and oh so full of hope that I can hardly face it.

Instead, I keep my voice light. I'm casual, I think. Impervious.

"Sure," I say. "You can stay the night."

But he corrects me, almost immediately.

"I don't mean just tonight," he says, as casual as I was. Like he's talking about the weather. "I mean always."

And then I realize.

He's done.

WILCO

Christine d'Abo

Lucy always found it amusing when submissives discovered she was in the navy. Especially if the men turned out to have a uniform fetish and begged her to wear it. Not that she ever did, but those nights were usually entertaining. Her khakis were currently neatly folded and tucked away back at her apartment away from any prying eyes. Tonight wasn't about that part of her life. And while many would argue she was simply trading one uniform for another, Lucy knew it wasn't that simple.

She *needed* this.

The hem of the PVC skirt clung to her thighs as she made a circle around the club. It had been a few months since she'd been able to wear this outfit and her body had forgotten how to move in the material. Her ankles wobbled ever so slightly in the spike-heeled boots and her face itched beneath the leather mask she wore to hide her identity. This wasn't simply a costume, it was a refuge from the daily pressures of constantly taking orders. The never-ending press of bowing to someone else's will day in and day out made it necessary for Lucy to find an outlet for her naturally dominant tendencies where and when she could.

Her friends and family understood that it was a challenge for any woman in the military, but she knew they didn't appreciate the reasons why it was especially hard for her. Lucy *needed* to have a degree of control over her life. The past two months had made it impossible for her to have that control—until now.

The music in the club made it challenging to have a decent conversation, but she wasn't interested in chitchat. She stuck mostly to the bar, wishing not for the first time that it wasn't dry, and watched the male submissives do what they could to get her attention. They were mostly guys around her age, but no one really captured her interest. This was her first visit to the Leather Slipper in months and she was hoping to find what she craved: someone strong and confident, someone she could take down a few pegs.

Finishing her Coke, Lucy was about to leave when a new arrival caught her eye. For a moment, she thought she must be imagining things because there was no way *he* could be here. Lucy wasn't sure if Commander Tyler Richardson even knew what sex was, let alone what went on in a place like this.

The next thought was that her former boss was here looking for her.

But that was impossible.

Lucy brushed her fingers along the edge of her mask, reassuring herself that it was securely in place. Originally, she'd taken to wearing it to hide her youth from those who wouldn't expect her to have the level of control necessary to meet their needs. She'd continued to wear it long past the time it was necessary, as others came to expect it to as part of her persona.

Now it would act as a shield, protecting her identity from the man who'd helped make her the officer she was now. The man who made her pussy clench and her breasts ache simply by entering the room.

The last thing Lucy wanted was for Richardson to recognize her. She had a hard enough time when it came to some of the ribbing she took from some of the male officers without adding the fact that she was a dominatrix into the mix.

The commander was dressed in civvies, making him look a lot younger than his forty years. The black T-shirt he wore clung perfectly to his shoulders and chest, showing off the fit body she'd caught a glimpse of once after they'd gotten soaked during a training exercise. He was in better shape than most of the twenty-something-year-old junior officers of her acquaintance.

Lucy's nails dug into her palm as she watched him survey the room. Then his gaze landed on her. It had been over a year since she'd seen him last, when he'd transferred to shore duty. There didn't seem to be any hint of recognition on his face, nor did he make any move to come closer. He simply stood there and stared. It took every ounce of her control not to squirm under the directness of his gaze. They weren't back on base, and within these walls she wasn't a subordinate. It didn't matter who they were in the harsh light of day; here at the Leather Slipper, Lucy was in charge. The fissure of tension quickly dissipated.

She was about to get up and confront him when a woman who Lucy knew to be a submissive slid up to Richardson and gently took his hand. She lifted it to her face and rained kisses along the back of his knuckles. Instead of the smirk she'd grown used to seeing, Lucy was surprised when he jerked his hand away and shook his head.

He wasn't here to find a sub? Then what the hell did he want?

The woman scurried away and Richardson went back to staring at Lucy.

Lucy didn't realize she was moving until she was halfway across the room. He never once looked away from her, even when she cut across the open dance floor through the crowd of writhing bodies. His eyes widened then, presumably because he got the full effect of her black PVC corset and skirt, but otherwise he didn't make a move.

She wore her hair down, the loose curls covering her shoulders, so very unlike the tight bun she was forced to wear during the workday. In her boots, Lucy came up to be almost equal to his six-foot frame, putting her on a far more level playing field than she was used to having with him.

Jutting her hip out to the side, she crossed her arms and peered at him from behind the mask. "Army boy?"

She could have laughed as he stiffened, his chin jutting out slightly. "Navy."

Lucy snorted. "Of course you are."

"Not hard to guess, living in this town." His normally deep voice sounded rougher than normal. "Interesting place."

"You're clearly new. Who's your sponsor?" Someone had to have gotten him in. Finding out who might raise some interesting questions.

Richardson laced his hands behind his back and widened his stance ever so slightly. "I'm a friend of the owner."

God, if Lucy had known that, she would have picked another club. Too many nights she'd spent fantasizing about this man, picturing him falling to his knees, shirt off, waiting for her to tell him to get naked. She'd dreamed of taking the belt from his service khakis and beating his ass red until he begged her to let him fuck her.

It had taken her weeks to rid her fantasies of that particular image.

"So, navy boy, why are you here?"

His gaze slid from hers to a spot above her shoulder. "I'm looking for...for someone, Ma'am."

Lucy cocked an eyebrow. Reaching out, she took him by the chin and forced him to look at her. "Who?"

She almost didn't believe him when he let his gaze pointedly drop from hers to the floor. His tongue darted out to wet his lips and, for the first time since her acquaintance with the commander, he looked nervous.

"You, Ma'am."

The thrill that raced through Lucy was nearly enough to make her come on the spot. No, he couldn't actually mean her. He was simply looking for a domme, someone he could play around with. But even that felt wrong. Richardson never once gave her the submissive vibe, and Lucy had long ago figured out how to pick one out at a hundred paces. There was something else going on and she was determined to find out what.

"Why the hell should I waste my time with the likes of you?"

He opened his mouth to speak, but nothing came out. It was the first time Lucy had ever seen him tongue-tied. He was a fast thinker, quick to toss off a smart-ass remark meant to put junior officers in their place. Not once had she seen him stumble. Not until now.

Lucy knew she needed to give him time to process things. Richardson might not even know himself why he had been driven to come here. He wouldn't be the first person to come to a club like this seeking answers to questions he didn't fully understand.

He pulled his shoulders back and lifted his chin, but kept his gaze on the floor. "Ma'am, I've recently had some things change in my life. I need...to understand."

"Understand what?"

"I..." He growled softly. "I don't rightfully know."

If she was thinking straight, Lucy would turn around and let him find someone else to show him how glorious it could be to give up control. She couldn't get involved with a superior officer. Had it been any other man, that's exactly what she would have done. Instead, Lucy circled his throat with her hand, digging her nails into the soft skin and feeling his pulse pounding beneath her fingers. She'd wanted him since the first day she'd seen him. Knew there could be something between them if they tried.

"You come with me and I expect your total obedience. I'm not one of your minions who will scurry off to do your bidding at the snap of your fingers. This is my domain, and in here I'm the boss. Do you understand, sailor boy?"

"Yes, Ma'am."

Lucy didn't need to tell him to follow her. They all did when they got to this point in the game. She made her way over to Brandon, one of the dungeon monitors standing along the back of the room near the bar. The man paid no attention to Richardson, though Lucy could tell he was checking him out nonetheless.

"I see you've found some fun for the night, Mistress Rose."

She'd chosen to use her middle name when she started coming to the Slipper. Now she was grateful she'd had the foresight to do so. "Yes, Brandon. Are there any rooms available?"

As Brandon took a quick look at the list, Lucy felt Richardson slide up behind her. It was so close to her fantasies that she was barely able to suppress a shiver. Turning her head to look at him from over her shoulder, she bit off a quick "Three steps back, sailor." It was gratifying to see him comply as quickly as he did.

Brandon was smirking when Lucy turned around once more. "You're in luck. The gray room is now free. You and your friend can use it."

"Thank you, love." She patted his chest as she strolled by. "I'll be a while."

"I have no doubt, Mistress. Enjoy your toy."

The air in the room was cool when she entered. Her nipples tightened beneath the PVC, and goose bumps rose along her arms even as she moved about. It wouldn't be long before she'd warm up, though. Sitting down on the lounge along the back of the room, she waited for Richardson to look his fill of the surroundings.

The room itself was relatively spartan. The gray walls gave the room its name, but the restraints along the wall needed little adornment to draw attention to them. Richardson walked over to one set of chains and fingered the cuffs.

"So this is what you do here? Tie men up?"

"Not just me." Lucy tugged the hem of her skirt. "And it's not always about being restrained. What is it that appeals to you?"

She knew he was still finding his way, but she had to know the direction of his thoughts if she was going to make this work. Still, it was more shocking to hear him speak the words than she'd ever experienced from any other sub.

"I need someone to control me." The way he spoke sounded like each syllable was spoken through a mouth full of glass.

"Control has many faces. I can tell you what to do, when and how to do it." Lucy licked her lips as she slid her hand across her thigh. His attention shifted from the leather cuffs to her hand. "I can command you the way they do in your precious navy. Would you like that?"

He didn't speak. She had no doubt he didn't even know what he was feeling at this point, let alone how to express it. He looked away and pinched the bridge of his nose. The frown on his face nearly broke her heart. For half a second she considered ripping off her mask to let him know that she was there—not Mistress Rose, but Lucy. There'd always been a connection between them, even when there shouldn't have been. It was wrong to have these types of feelings for one's commanding officer.

Lucy didn't care.

"In this world there are rules. I think a sailor like you would be used to that." Lucy slipped from her perch and approached him cautiously. "Unlike your world, it's usually the one on the receiving end who gets to call the shots."

He nodded. "I'm not sure if I'm into pain. I see enough of that every day."

Disappointing, but if this turned out to be more than a one-night event, then Lucy had the chance to introduce him to the idea. "So what is it you want?" Reaching up, she fingered the hem of his T-shirt. "Do you want me to take control? Tell you what to do? Make everything nice and simple?"

The nod when it came was barely perceptible. Right. Richardson spent day in and day out controlling the fates of others. It was his words, his training that ensured that the men and women who crossed his path were ready to face the challenges that service life presented them. It stood to reason that he would get off on someone else taking control, putting him through the wringer and ensuring his pleasure.

Yeah, that she could do.

"If I do something you don't like I want you to say *red*. Not *stop* or *don't*. *Red*." He nodded. Lucy came to stand behind him. He hadn't released his grip on the leather cuff and she knew he was using it as a means to ground himself. "I want you to raise your hands above your head and face me."

This wasn't about asking permission. And though she didn't know exactly what he was trying to get out of tonight, she knew where they could start. Lucy took a step back and waited to see what he would do. Instead of complying with her command, he reached out and fingered the side of her mask. "Why do you wear this?"

Lucy ignored the way her heart pounded at the briefest of caresses, his fingers against her cheek. "I'm the one in control. I ask the questions. Now do what I say, or else leave."

She didn't think he'd do it. Not really. So when he lifted his hands above his head and took a step back so he was now pressed against the wall, her breath caught in her lungs. This time Lucy held his gaze as she lifted the cuffs and secured first one, then the other around his wrists. The silver chains shone in the dim light as he tested them out. There wasn't enough length to give him much room to move, but it would be enough for Lucy to twist and turn him as she wanted.

"It's a shame I didn't tell you to take your shirt off first. Not that I plan to deprive myself of the sight of your chest." Grabbing the hem of his T-shirt, she lifted it up and over his head until it was bunched behind his neck. The stretched fabric further served to restrict his movements while at the same time framing his flawless torso.

"What do you do in the navy?"

"I was in surface warfare, a commander."

Lucy froze. "Was?"

"I took the option of early retirement." Richardson looked away, exposing the side of his jaw and the muscle twitching beneath the surface. "I couldn't do it anymore."

Of all the reasons he could have come here tonight, that was the last one she would have suspected. "And where do you plan to go from here?"

"I'm not sure. I feel like I'm..."

"Adrift?"

The look of relief on his face was one Lucy wouldn't soon

forget. "Yes. I've been fighting against something I don't quite understand for a long time. I couldn't do anything about it in the navy."

That he was in pain and Lucy could help him set her heart racing again. She understood what it was like to be trapped like that. Wanting to be a part of something larger than oneself and yet needing to protect a piece of your soul to stay sane. Lucy was still struggling to find a way to make that happen. Clearly, he was ready to find his path.

They were opposite sides of the same coin—power and influence reversed from what they both needed. Lucy raked her nails down his naked chest. She grazed his nipples, smiling when he sucked in a sharp breath.

"You like that."

"Yes, Ma'am."

"Normally I prefer my subs to call me Mistress, but Ma'am sounds right coming from you. You keep saying that."

"Yes," he sucked in another breath as Lucy tweaked his nipple, "Ma'am."

"I'm going to play now. You stand still, sailor."

Lucy continued to rake her nails up and down the length of his torso. She took her time exploring the expanse of skin before her, needing to learn the landscape so she could make his blood sing. Her mouth watered as she lowered her lips to his chest. She knew he could take the pain and held nothing back as she nipped and bit his skin. He flinched, his hands wrapping around the chains that held him, but he didn't try to twist away.

"You're gorgeous. But I bet you know that. I bet you spent your days teasing all the women on your ship and around your base." She reached around and grabbed his ass. "I bet you shook this in the faces of all those pretty young things, knowing they could never get you."

"No, Ma'am. I wouldn't do that."

"You wouldn't?" Lucy leaned in and bit down on his cloth-covered shoulder. "I find that hard to believe. You would enjoy teasing those girls, make them want you even when they knew they couldn't touch you."

"Ma'am, no—"

Lucy dropped to her knees, her face level with his groin. "Shut up."

He groaned, this time jerking hard on the chains when she leaned forward and pressed her face to his covered erection. "Shouldn't I be doing something for you?"

"If I wanted something, then I would tell you." Lucy blew hot air across his shaft. He groaned and bucked his hips forward. She repeated the action, this time smiling as her red lipstick smudged the fabric. "Right now I want this."

She quickly fumbled with the buckle on his belt, jerking it, along with the front of his pants, open. "I want to see what you're packing, sailor."

"Yes, Ma'am." His eyes were screwed shut, and he was breathing out in sharp gasps. "Fuck."

Lucy reached in and pulled his cock out, exposing his hot shaft to the air. Curling her fingers around him, she rose back to her feet. The weight of his pants pulled them down his legs, and with only a little help from her, they slipped down to pool around his feet.

"Bend your knees so it's sticking out."

He was slow to comply, though Lucy suspected his delay had more to do with the lustful haze he was now under and not from any insubordination. With a move far more awkward than it should have been, Lucy pulled up her skirt with one hand as she straddled his thigh. She'd forgone panties, loving the feel of the PVC against her shaved pussy. She was wet and her clit throbbed from her desire for him.

She gave his cock a squeeze as she ground down on his thigh. They both groaned, their voices echoing off the walls. "Don't you dare come. Not until I tell you to."

"Shit," he muttered, only to gasp when she tugged down on his balls. "God, yes, Ma'am."

"Yes, Ma'am what?"

"I won't come until you tell me to."

Lucy's heart raced as she rubbed herself off on his leg. Despite her pleasurable distraction, she continued to listen to the staccato rhythm of his breathing. He jerked and twisted in his chains as she pumped his cock in time with her thrusts. It took an embarrassingly short amount of time for her to feel her orgasm approach. Leaning in, she sucked on his nipple, worrying the skin with her teeth.

"God, Lucy."

She jerked her head up, and even though she now pressed down hard on his leg, her attention was solely fixed on his face. "What?"

His eyes were closed, but he opened them wide in surprise. "What? Ma'am?"

Lucy squeezed his cock, but she was too far gone to stop now. "Say it again."

He licked his lips, gasping on her up stroke. "Lucy. Please, Lucy. I want to come. Want *you* to come."

That was it. Closing her eyes, she ground down on his thigh one more time and let her orgasm wash over her. Her skin ignited as she finally gave in to months of sexual frustration, each cell tingling with pleasure as wave after wave of pleasure blanked out the world around her. When everything finally stilled and she came back to herself, Lucy was clinging to his body, his hard cock still in her hand.

"When did you know it was me?"

"Lucy—"

"When?" She gave his shaft a hard tug. "*When?*"

He licked his lips before lowering his chin to his chest. "Four or five months ago."

"What?" No, that was impossible.

"I was curious about this place. I saw you walk in. I watched you."

Lucy let her hand slip lower and cupped his balls. "I never saw you. I...wanted you."

"Please let me come, Lucy." She tugged on his sac. "Ma'am! God, please."

"Why didn't you seek me out before now?" None of this made any sense to her. He had never once expressed any interest in her when they worked together. Not that he could, not while he was still her superior....

Lucy dropped to her knees and held her mouth an inch above the head of his cock. "Tyler, tell me."

"I needed to make sure." He was openly panting now, his chest rising and falling like a billow. "After that first night I couldn't get the image of you dressed like this out of my head. I kept having dreams of you standing over me, making me beg you for it, spanking me." A deep blush covered his face, though if it was a result of embarrassment or lust Lucy wasn't sure.

She held his gaze as she lowered her mouth to the tip. "Only come when I say."

He nodded frantically, even as she sucked the tip deep into her mouth. His skin was hot and tasted of precome. The scent of his arousal had her pussy clenching in renewed interest. She knew when the time came she'd ride his cock until they were both screaming for release. But not now.

Sucking him down to the root of his shaft, Lucy kept her

gaze on his. It didn't take long to know he'd be unable to hold out any longer. She pulled off just long enough to whisper a harsh "Now."

This time when she took him in her mouth, he thrust deep. Once, twice and he was coming hard into her mouth. The muscles in his thighs shook and she could feel the vibrations carry up into his stomach muscles. She swallowed down every ounce of his release and licked him clean.

He was sagging in the chains, his arms pulling against the cuffs. Knowing he'd be in pain if she didn't get him down soon, Lucy pulled herself together long enough to free him and help him to the floor. They sat side by side, surrounded by the sounds of their breathing and the smell of sex.

"Why did you retire?" she asked after the silence stretched to uncomfortable lengths.

He turned his head and stared at her. Without warning, he reached over and took her hand. "I've been unhappy for a while now. Not that anything was really wrong, but I think I was ready for a change."

"And me?" She almost didn't want to ask, scared of what the answer might be.

"I would never have taken advantage of anyone under my command—or even after I left the ship." He reached over and pulled the mask from her face. "Even a woman like you who is more than capable of looking after herself and everyone else around her. I've been attracted to you ever since I met you, and I wanted to be with you."

"You left the navy because of me?"

He shrugged. "I left because you were the first woman who I knew would understand what I needed. I knew it was time to take a chance."

"I..." She swallowed past the unexpected lump in her throat.

"I want to take that chance. I've been looking for someone too."

"Me?"

She nodded. "If you think you can put up with me."

Tyler smiled for the first time that night. "Oh, yes, Ma'am."

CHRISTMAS
PRESENTS

Mercy Loomis

S o what are you doing for Christmas?" Chi asked.

Robbie Bairns didn't glance up from the rifle barrel he was swabbing out. "Nothing."

Chi frowned at him before sighting down the barrel of his own weapon. "Nothing? You're not going home?" He grimaced at the dirt and picked up the cloth again. "Doing anything for New Year's, then? Going to party like it's 1999 because it finally *will* be 1999?"

"Nope." Robbie tried not to let anything show, but he felt his jaw clench. There was only so much pretending he was capable of.

It was different here on base, like a whole other world. The frustration was easier to bear, even if he couldn't talk to his buddies about it. At home he'd had Cassie, true. But here, he had brothers. He'd never had brothers.

He had a sister, Amanda, but he'd never told her, either. Just Cassie.

Chi didn't look up from the metal in his hands, but his attention widened, somehow. Chi was good at shit like that. He could walk into a room and you just felt him secure the perimeter, set sentries. Chi always had your back.

"You want to talk about it?" Chi asked quietly.

Robbie shrugged. "Not much there, honestly. My mom, she's real intense, you know? She's always wanted me to be successful, but like in business or something." He shook his head. "I think she's finally squared with me enlisting, but now she wants me to get promoted. It gets heavy. And Mom and my sister are constantly fighting."

"Sucks." Chi would've sounded more sympathetic if Robbie had scuffed his dress boots. For some reason, that lack of emotional response always made Robbie feel better. It sort of reminded him of his dad. Stoic and unruffled. Robbie had always tried to emulate that, but it never went more than skin deep.

"I mean, I do miss them and all. But I'd rather see them separately than all at once." Robbie tried to laugh, but it came out a little flat.

"Sure. I get that." Chi checked the barrel one more time and gave a satisfied grunt.

For a moment the only noise was the soft clink of metal against metal as Chi began reassembling the M16. Robbie couldn't stop himself from stealing a look. There shouldn't be anything wrong with a look, right? Just a glance. Totally casual.

Chi had the hottest hands of anyone Robbie had ever met. Sure, the guy was buff, too, but who wasn't, around here? Robbie had never thought he'd be attracted to someone's hands, but his friend had such long, slender fingers, quick and dexterous, flying over the parts laid out next to him, plucking them up and slotting them into place. It was like watching a street magician doing coin tricks.

Robbie forced his attention back to his own weapon. *Stop that,* he berated himself. Chi was his friend. Maybe his best friend. The last thing Robbie wanted was another unrequited crush. He'd had enough of those in high school.

Okay, not the last thing. The next to last thing.

I don't want to get kicked out.

"You know," Chi said, startling Robbie out of his dark thoughts, "my folks are going to be visiting my grandparents in Japan. I'm kinda at loose ends, too. You want to spend your vacation at my place?"

That was a solution Robbie had never considered. All their friends had been talking about going to see their families, but now that he thought about it, Chi had been about as silent on the subject as Robbie had been.

"Yeah." Robbie's response was a little timid, but Chi's grin set him at ease. Chi looked genuinely relieved at not being left alone for Christmas. "Yeah, that would be awesome. Thanks, man."

Robbie set his duffel down on the bed and looked the room over. It was light and airy: huge window with gauzy white curtains, the walls and ceiling painted in cool ocean blues and greens, the few decorations mostly white with splashes of seashell pinks and oranges.

Chi walked to the window and slid it open, letting in a breeze to make the curtains billow. A warm breeze. In December.

"I cannot believe I'm in Hawaii," Robbie said, coming over to the window and looking out. "This place is like a movie set."

"A little different from home, eh, Backwater?"

"I'll say. We don't get above freezing much this time of year in Wisconsin."

"Ugh." Chi shuddered dramatically. "I can't imagine. Cold and I do not get along." He turned away from the window and gave Robbie a once-over. "That was a helluva long flight. Wanna hit the hot tub and unwind?"

"You have a hot tub, too?" Shit, was he dreaming?

"Yeah, we have a hot tub. What's the point of living in this climate if you don't have a hot tub?"

Robbie hadn't brought any trunks—the only ones he owned were back in Wisconsin—but Chi loaned him a pair. Feeling awkward, Robbie retreated to the guest room to change. It was weird. He'd seen Chi naked before, of course. He'd seen pretty much his entire unit naked, but when he was on base he'd just ignored it. He was on the job, on base. He was a professional, damn it, and he made sure he acted like one.

And being absolutely terrified of being outed tended to put a damper on one's libido, anyway.

But this wasn't base.

Stop that.

Robbie met Chi in the kitchen and followed him out onto the deck, where a four-person hot tub sat waiting. Chi pulled the cover off, and the two men sank into the hot water.

"I could get used to this," Robbie muttered. He leaned back into the headrest and closed his eyes, listening to the whirring of the motor and the burbling of the water and the distant, hypnotic rhythm of waves on the shore.

"So what's your girlfriend think of you not coming home?"

"What? Oh, Cassie?" Robbie shrugged. "She's fine. She wasn't going home, either."

"Uh-huh." Chi sounded doubtful. "Anything you want to talk about?"

Everything.

Robbie tried not to let his expression change. He was so tired.

The long flight, the excitement of the trip and this wonderful hot tub were conspiring against him. It was only in finally relaxing that he realized how tight he'd been wound.

I want to talk about everything. I don't want to feel so alone.

"I miss Cassie," he murmured.

"You don't call her much."

What's the point? I can't talk about any of that on a military phone. Ever since they'd passed Don't Ask, Don't Tell a few years ago, witch hunts had been rife. The wrong word, the wrong tone of voice, a careless email, logging into the wrong website...any of it would be enough to start an investigation. He'd seen it happen.

"She's in pre-med. She's busy."

"Does she know you don't love her?"

Robbie's head snapped up, a sharp retort already forming on his lips, but Chi's expression stopped him. Chi looked...sad? It wasn't pity; more like empathy. It pulled some of the anger out of Robbie. Chi was a charmer, quiet but witty, but now all of his levity was gone. Robbie had never seen him look so serious.

"I do love her. Just not like that. And yeah, she knows."

He wasn't sure why he said it, other than Chi's expression demanded an answer. He'd meant to leave it at that, but it was like the words had been the plug, and now the pressure had an outlet.

"She was the cheer captain. I was the quarterback. Everyone just assumed we'd date, you know? And Cassie didn't want to get tied down in that stupid little town. Neither did I." Robbie laughed. "Man, you should meet her. She's like a fucking missile. Locked on target, get out of her way."

"So why did you guys date?"

Robbie rolled his eyes. "To keep everyone else from bugging us."

Chi snorted. "You think you're that hot?"

"Everyone loves the quarterback."

Except the guys. Fuck, if they'd known they were showering with a gay guy...

"So she covered for you, and you kept the hicks away from her." Chi cocked his head thoughtfully. "Not a bad deal."

Robbie pretended to ignore the comment, but the bottom dropped out of his stomach. Had he said too much? He ran back over the conversation frantically, searching for anything he'd let slip. It all sounded innocuous enough to him.

"Of course, I suppose it doesn't help your egotism that you *are* that hot."

Did he just say that?

Robbie blinked at him. "Uh. Thanks?"

It was Chi's turn to roll his eyes. "Robbie, have you not figured it out yet? I'm gay, too."

Robbie stared. "I...uh, I'm not—"

Before Robbie could think how to react, Chi leaned forward, grabbed him by the ears and kissed him hard.

Robbie responded instinctively, his mind going blank as soon as he felt Chi's lips on his. His eyes closed, his mouth opened and his heart twisted violently in his chest, hope and terror and longing choking him. He only realized how hard he was kissing Chi back when his friend broke away with a breathless laugh.

"Trust me, no straight man kisses that well."

Robbie hardly heard him. His mind was so blown his ears were buzzing. "Do that again?"

Chi grinned, and there was the mischievous light that Robbie had seen in his eyes so many times, but it was edgier now, heavier. "Gladly," Chi replied, tracing Robbie's lower lip with one finger, "but we should probably go inside. We don't have a privacy fence and I haven't told my parents yet."

Inside. Robbie had never heard such a beautiful word before. "Right. Yeah. Sure." He sloshed his way out of the hot tub, following Chi, hardly feeling the cooler air on his wet skin as he trotted across the deck and into the kitchen.

Chi started to head down the hall, but Robbie grabbed his arm. "Wait," he said, desperately trying to get his brain working again. "You're really...you're not just fucking with me or something, right?"

Chi took Robbie's free hand and pressed himself against it, molding Robbie's fingers around his hard cock. "Does it feel like I'm just fucking with you?"

Robbie's balls grew so tight they actually hurt. He squeezed, the wet cloth of Chi's swim trunks bunching against his palm. Chi's eyelids fluttered a little, his breath hissing between his teeth, and that look of pleasure made Robbie's mind go blank again. He brought his mouth down on Chi's, demanding and hungry, a continuous assault that Chi returned in kind, Chi's hands slipping under Robbie's trunks, grabbing his ass, pulling him close until Robbie's erection was trapped against Chi's hip.

"Oh, *god,*" Robbie gasped, arching his back.

Chi shook himself, pushed away. "Bedroom," he muttered, sounding a bit dazed. He removed his hands from Robbie's swimsuit and took a step back, drawing Robbie with him. "Bedroom. Condoms are in the bedroom."

"Right, right." Robbie's head spun as if he were drunk. "Good call."

He didn't remember the trip down the hall. The next thing he saw was Chi standing in front of his bed, stripping off his wet trunks.

For the first time, Robbie let himself look, really look. It was like on TV where they blurred out the good bits, only now the blur had been removed. Chi's dusky skin was nearly dry, but water still ran in little rivulets down his muscular legs and that lovely little crease where thigh met pelvis...then Chi ran a hand lightly over himself and Robbie thought his knees might give out.

"You gonna make me do this myself?" Chi quipped. "Or are you gonna get your ass over here?"

Robbie whipped off the swim trunks while Chi laughed. He held out his hand for the condom Chi was holding.

"I'm half surprised you know what to do with that, Backwater."

"I'm not completely ignorant, hippie boy." Robbie tried to keep his hands from shaking as he tore open the foil. He pushed Chi back until the other man sat down, then knelt between his legs. Robbie buried his face in the hollow just below Chi's hip, Chi's balls brushing his cheek, tight and wrinkled and oh so soft.

I don't even know what they call this bit of anatomy, Robbie thought as he licked beads of water off Chi's thigh. He hardly noticed the chlorine. *Whatever it's called, I love it. Love it, love it, love it.*

"Oh, hell," Chi hissed, throwing his head back as Robbie rolled the condom on. "I have been wanting you to do that for months."

Robbie laughed into Chi's thigh, then turned his head and ran his tongue down the length of Chi's erection. The texture of the latex was almost harsh after Chi's skin, but that wasn't important. What was important was the sound Chi made and the way his cock jumped under Robbie's mouth.

Chi swore. "You keep that up and I'm not going to last. Get up here."

Robbie crawled onto the bed, already so hard he wasn't sure he could handle Chi putting the condom on him. But he gritted his teeth and breathed through it, and they spent some time exploring each other in different ways, lips and hands stroking and caressing, and the kissing, god, long, slow, passionate kisses that made Robbie's nerve endings sing until he couldn't stand it anymore.

He reached between them, wrapping one hand around Chi's shaft, squeezing, and Chi moaned into his mouth, the vibration of that sound seeming to travel all through him. And then the pressure of a hand on his own cock, those slender, clever fingers playing him like an instrument, coaxing the orgasm out of him like a street magician conjures a coin.

Afterward, they lay together, spent and happily entwined, Chi's head resting on Robbie's shoulder, Chi's buzzed black hair tickling Robbie's cheek.

"And we have another week here?" Robbie asked dazedly.

"Yep." Chi snuggled a little closer and gave a contented sigh.

They'd have to be careful once they were back on base, of course. But they'd make it work. They already spent most of their time together, and there would be leave days off base when they could be amorous even if they had to be hands-off the rest of the time.

But first, a whole week alone together before heading home.

Home. Because the army was home. His unit was all the family he needed. The army, and this guy right here.

Robbie smiled and kissed the top of Chi's head. "Best. Christmas. Ever."

SNAKE DANCE

Lynn Townsend

Airman Mitchell Llewellyn was going to throw up. He bent over, nearly doubled in his seat. If he was lucky he would manage to vomit all over the floor in front of him and keep his boots out of it and the only thing that would come of it—aside from probably being thrown out of the club—was that his squad would never let him forget it. He'd end up with a flight name like Cookies or something equally humiliating, but it would go away soon enough. His wingman's call sign was Conman, and the less said about that, the better.

If he wasn't lucky, he'd manage to soak his jeans and boots. It was nearly an hour's car ride back to their hotel. He'd not expected that Vegas was so large; it was a single city, in the middle of the desert. How could anything be so far away from anything else? With the traffic, he'd be lucky if they made it back to the shower before three in the morning. Mitch had heard New York described as the city that never slept, but Vegas? Vegas didn't even know the meaning of sleep. The city ran on booze, sex and 5-hour Energy.

If he was very unlucky, and he was currently entertaining the possibility of extreme karmic retribution, he'd lose his lunch—what lunch? Had he actually eaten any lunch at all?—all over his squad leader. Yeah, that'd be just peachy. Not like Peterson liked him much anyway. This was just going to seal his fate if he upchucked a stomach full of cheap beer and bar nuts all over Peterson's fancy leave duds.

Would it be so bad, he wondered, if he just fell onto the floor? Maybe his roiling stomach would ease. Or at least, he'd not splash quite so badly when he lost it.

He kept his gaze firmly on the floor and counted backward, a trick his mother had taught his sisters. His mom was a career pregnant woman; with Mitch as the second oldest child with seven sisters between him and his younger brother, he'd heard a lot from his mother about pregnancy, morning sickness and all the things that had made him squirm with embarrassment at the time.

"Hey, sailor."

A foot appeared in his line of sight, perfectly formed with delicate toes painted an impossible shade of green. He knew it was perfect because the shoe that enclosed it was entirely made of glass. Well, plastic probably. A massive platform heel, the sort you saw in porn videos, with a fish swimming around in the toe. Not a fish, a decoration, but still, it undulated gently in the water, looking peaceful.

"...airman..." Mitch muttered to the shoe.

Fascinating. How did the owner of that delicate foot actually walk in those shoes? He never could figure out why women did it—except that men enjoyed the effects of heels on the legs and ass of a woman. Seemed like a sucky reason to so thoroughly abuse one's feet, but hey, if they didn't mind, he wasn't going to object.

"I'm a naval aviator."

"Whatever."

Perfect foot was attached to perfect leg. Short skirt—so short
it should be illegal. Wasn't even a skirt at all, just a couple of
flaps of brilliant green tied over her hips. Bare midriff. Mitch
raised his eyes further. An olive-sized glass gem set in her navel,
glinting wickedly in the sea of her flat, naked belly. Two scraps of
green cloth, sequined with black tassels hanging down, cupped
a pair of average, but very nice, breasts.

"Hey, the eyes are up here, Airman."

"Yeah," Mitch said. "I know. Just taking the scenic route."

"Take your time," she said. She shifted her weight—or maybe
the weight of that tray of drinks—which did interesting things
to her hips. "I ain't going nowhere."

"What's the problem, ma'am?" Mitch managed to jerk his
eyes the rest of the way up, focusing solely on the waitress's face,
and ignoring as best he could the show in the background, that
terrible display that was making him so sick to begin with. "We
didn't order another round."

"Oh, that's all right, I'll take it out in trade. You can work
it off."

"Huh?"

"Come with me, Airman." She leaned down to whisper in
his ear, giving him a long, leisurely look down her shirt. She
straightened, then distributed the beers to his squad. "On the
house, boys," she said, passing them out. "Drink up. We're all
so grateful to our servicemen and women, you know. Keep this
country great!"

His squad didn't ask questions. Free beer was free beer.
And it wouldn't be the first time some retired navy captain
had bought them a round or someone had treated them to
dinner in memory of their brother who'd died over there in that

godforsaken desert. If there was someone to thank, thanks were
given. But free booze, free food and one time a complimentary
limo ride, these gifts were never, ever refused. It was rude. And
you know the military and free beer. Like peanut butter and
jelly. Apple pie and ice cream.

Mitch swayed alarmingly as he got to his feet. He hadn't had
that many drinks, but the show, oh mother Mary of god, the
show; he was going to vomit, and now karma really was being a
cunt because he was going to vomit all over the pretty waitress.

"This way, darlin'," she said. She grabbed his arm, her fingers
cool on his overheated skin, and turned him expertly away from
the stage. At that point he would have followed her into hell just
to get away.

The guy in the front row was going to toss his cookies. That
was as obvious to her as it was to Seth, the bartender. Not that
it was unusual. They were a bar, and they were a strip club and
there was more alcohol under this roof than should be allowed.
Vomit was just a part of bar life. But usually it was contained
to the bathroom or that small, overcrowded hall that led to the
restrooms. And it was never Mandu's concern. She was a waitress, not part of the cleaning crew.

But there was something about this guy; he went ash pale
as soon as Medusa had started her act, bringing Reggie out to
dance with her. It wasn't the first time Mandu had seen that
look on a man's face. Innermost Fantasies promised the most
exotic, the most wild, the most unique nude entertainment on
the strip. Well, exotic it was. Wild, yeah, that too. Unique?
Probably not. Freak shows of the less naked variety had been
common as long as there had been people stupid enough to lay
down their money.

And yet, pale as he was and in danger of puking, the guy

stayed firmly in his seat, swallowing excess saliva and keeping his eyes averted. Medusa—her real name was of the less exotic variety, Dee Dee Simpson—was actually one of the more mild dancers, her lithe, curvy body moving in time with the music, the rasp of her partner's flesh against her own still somehow audible, even over the crushing beat and the rowdy crowd.

Reggie was a snake. A sixteen-foot-long boa python with marbled skin and a flat, evil, wedge-shaped head. Tame, mind you, for the Innermost.

Other nights, the headline acts included blood-play, various B&D shows, pony-play, and other, even more deviant performances. Dee Dee and her snake, even as the python twisted over her naked body, sticking his nose and tongue along her flesh, tasting and smelling the snake urine that Dee Dee daubed on her skin to get his attention, hadn't bothered her much, even when she'd first started to work at Innermost. Not that she'd particularly wanted Reggie to slither over her, but the snake was old, slow, well-trained and vastly overfed. He wasn't interested in eating anyone.

That aside, there was something about the boy. And he really did look like a boy with that ridiculous military haircut and fashion sense that looked like it came out of a J.Crew catalog. A boy masquerading as a man who was determined to tough it out even if it was looking like he was going to lose that battle.

"Here I come to save the day," Mandu muttered.

She couldn't have said why she decided to get involved. Certainly no one in this city was a Good Samaritan, and after five years of living here, she'd rarely felt the need to do a good thing for anyone if it didn't involve a better tip. Maybe it was that boyish look; he seemed younger and more vulnerable than his friends, with wide blue eyes and a cleft chin. The sort of jutting chin one could rest a shot glass on, as Tina the hostess

often joked. Superman had a chin like that. The old Christopher
Reeve Superman, not that punk in the remake.

"Hey."

He looked up at her, blue eyes that were so lost, full of revul-
sion and terror. She knew she was doing the right thing.

With the patience of a saint, she managed to extricate him
from his friends, gently tugging him across the bar's slightly
sticky floor. He was so intent, staring anywhere but the stage
that he didn't even notice that she led him out of the bar. He
didn't look up until cold night air blew across his skin.

"What the hell?"

"You didn't look like you were enjoying the show."

"I wasn't. But what's it to you?"

"Maybe I have a soft spot for hard-luck cases," Mandu said.
"And I didn't want to have to mop the floor when you puked
on it."

"Was it that obvious?"

"Probably not to your friends, they were too busy looking
at boobs."

"Not usually something I'm averse to myself," he said. "My
name's Mitch, by the way. Thank you."

"Mandu," she introduced herself. "Which is not Mandy. I
ain't a Barry Manilow song." Too many dates played that song
for her, trying and failing to charm her.

"Mandu. Got it. So, you come here often?" Mitch gestured
at the alley. Away from the snake dancer, he appeared a little
more animated, and a lot more handsome than she'd actually
thought at first.

"Not usually, no. I don't smoke, but some of the girls do.
All the new laws, so they have to come out here to do it. It's
Thursday night and only Dee Dee still smokes; she's up on stage
now."

Mitch shuddered. "That was. Ugh. I know, it's unreasonable, I know. Less than ten thousand people a year are bitten by snakes, and of those less than a handful actually die. And that snake isn't even poisonous. I know it's stupid."

"You don't have to live through a plane crash to be afraid of flying," Mandu pointed out. "My brother was in the marines. Stay out here, ten, fifteen minutes. Dee Dee will be done, she'll go put Reggie away—"

"Reggie? That *thing* has a name? What is she, an Indiana Jones fan?"

"Something like that. You can tell your buds that I was so taken with you, I nailed you in the alley. I don't mind. That'll keep them from giving you hell about the snake. Save face."

Mandu hopped up onto the air generator. The rumble of the system vibrated pleasantly under her tired legs. She swung her feet, feeling the shock of relief, almost greater than the pain of walking around in those shoes all evening.

"You're doing all this for me? Why?"

"It's my break anyway."

She stared down at her feet enclosed in the clear shoes. Originally, she'd pitched the idea of doing a Cinderella act to the club's manager. The "talent" made the most money, not only from the bills given to them on the stage, but also they took a share of all the waitstaff's tips. But she wouldn't add throwing Tony a quick fuck on top of the pitch, so he'd let her wear her costume as a waitress, but not get up on the stage. Yay, life in Las Vegas. Totally glam.

Mitch stepped into the cradle of her legs, lifting her chin with one hand. "That's not really an answer." He was close, very close, and even in the cold desert air—why had no one told her how cold it got at night?—she could feel the heat radiating off his body. Mandu considered shoving him away; this was face saving, not an offer of a quick fuck, after all. She couldn't remember the last time she'd actually touched another person deliberately. Sought comfort from another human being. She leaned closer to him, resting her head against his broad chest.

"I wanted to do something nice for someone. Like no one ever does around here. You reminded me of me." She spoke to his shirt, a white linen button-down that smelled of generic fabric softener. "Like you'd come out here for something, found it entirely as you imagined it would be, and discovered that you actually didn't want it at all."

Mitch put his arms around her, fingers warm against the naked skin of her back. He rested his chin on top of her head and she felt suddenly protected there in the curve of his embrace. "This is nice," he said. "I haven't just talked to a girl in a long time. What'd you come out to Vegas looking for?"

"Not really sure. Glamorous life, maybe? My brother went and did something I thought was stupid, joined the marines while we're at war, and I guess I had to prove he wasn't the only idiot in the family. Only what he did was brave and wonderful, and what I did was just stupid."

"You said he was in the marines." Mitch's arms tightened around her. "What happened to him?"

"Yeah, 2nd battalion, tank division out of Lejeune. He was a gunner. He's home now. Honorably discharged. Purple Heart and all that." Tears prickled in her eyes. "He broke his back when some Iraqi threw a grenade at his jeep. He wasn't even in the tank, you know, just riding back to the base. He can walk now, a little, my mom says. I haven't been home to see him."

"Where's home?"

"Portsmouth, Virginia," Mandu said. "I doubt you've heard of it—"

"I have, actually. I'm stationed at Oceana," Mitch said. The door to the alley rattled, then opened.

"Small wor—" Mandu started to say, then Mitch's mouth descended on hers, swallowing her words. She froze, startled, then relaxed with a soft groan of desire as he tickled the edge of her lower lip with his tongue. *How strange,* she thought, barely coherent.

"Oh, sorry there, slick," one of the other airmen said, his face breaking out in a smirk. "Carry on."

"Go away, Conman," Mitch snarled, his lips twisting interestingly against Mandu's. She raised her legs, locked her ankles around the small of his back, pulling him closer. One hand dropped to her thigh, cupping the smooth skin. She writhed, pressing herself to him, need consuming the space between their bodies.

"Absolutely, Alleycat. Absolutely." Conman pointedly closed the door.

"Asshole," Mitch said, breathing hard. "I'm sorry, I just... wow, that was fine, though. I'm taking advantage of your kindness. I don't mean to be."

"Oh, shut up and kiss me again, Airman," Mandu said. Her legs remained locked around his hips and she rocked her pelvis against his. Delicious heat and a sudden, welcome hardness pressed between them.

"Yes, ma'am." Mitch grinned and bent to kiss her again. This time was slow, easy and gentle, just the barest hint of urgency, wanting, below the subtle dance of tongue and teeth. She tasted beer on his tongue, felt the curve of his lips against hers. Her fingers tightened on his shoulders and under the hard surface of his muscles she detected tremors of excitement.

Mandu lolled her head back and Mitch continued his exploration, his lips pressing against her cheek, nipping gently at her ear, then blazing a warm, wet trail down to her shoulder. His tongue found the sensitive spot along her collarbone and she groaned under the sensual onslaught.

It had been too long; she thrust her hips, too eager to be patient, too full of wanting and need to wait for him. Her panties, pale silvery briefs meant for show, chafed against the swollen flesh of her pussy. Rubbing aggravated the itch instead of relieving it. She hissed, her fingernails scoring along his neck. She raised her hands higher, feeling the rough scrub of his short military haircut against her palms as if somehow she had the power to hold him to her forever.

Mitch plunged one hand into her wealth of blond hair, tangling a fist near the nape of her neck. She gasped as he tugged lightly, tingles and prickles traveling down her scalp and spine.

"Do you like that?" he asked. Mandu tried to nod; constrained by his grip on her hair, she couldn't.

"Yes," she breathed.

"You want it?"

"Oh, yes."

Mitch kept her head captive, assaulting her throat and down the slope of her breast, his tongue wetting the thin material of her waitress costume. He blew warm air across the trail of wet, and while she couldn't see his face, she felt him smile against her skin as her flesh rippled with goose bumps, her nipples tightening behind the fabric.

She squirmed as he licked, tasting every inch of her exposed flesh and going nowhere near where she wanted. Mandu gasped, her voice breaking into a mewling cry of protest as he explored her belly, bypassed her hip and licked fire across her thigh. She was arched nearly double, elbows supporting her against the generator, breasts thrust out.

The hand in her hair hurt, it hurt, dammit, and her breasts hurt and her pussy ached. She couldn't move away from the assault of his mouth and didn't want to, but for god's sake he was torturing her. She cried out, locking her legs around his neck. The heels of her shoes tattooed against his back and he gripped one ankle with his free hand, holding that leg hostage as he licked again, delicate and sensual, against her thigh, just at the edge of those ridiculous panties.

The heat of his breath sent her into a gasping tremor, a rush of fluid dampening her panties. She clenched against a spasm that twisted through her belly. *I'm going to cream and he hasn't even touched me,* she thought, stunned.

"Stop fucking around and fuck me."

He relaxed his grip on her hair. Mandu sat up shivering, curling her arms around herself. Mitch sank onto one knee, his forehead against her pubic bone, the bridge of his nose settling against her slit. She stared down at his head in astonishment— he was vibrating!—and realized that it was laughter, soft but earnest, that shook him.

"Impatient, are you?"

She couldn't answer the obvious, just nodded.

"All right, then." He pulled back just long enough to yank her panties down, leaving them dangling from one ankle. He curled his arms around her thighs and lowered his head.

Mandu nearly screamed as his tongue touched her. Finally, finally, oh god, and then he was devouring her, licking and nibbling. She kept her pussy waxed, the panties were too sheer to allow for pubic hair, and her skin was so sensitive. She hissed and then whimpered as his tongue bathed over her sensitive flesh. She imagined that she could feel each taste bud on his tongue, each brush of his lip. His teeth found her swollen clit and the first bite was a stinging relief.

Mandu collapsed backward onto the generator, twisting her hips against him, spreading her legs to give him greater access.

He took it greedily, lapping at her thighs and the fold of her hip before returning to explore her pussy. One finger dipped into her slit, then a second. He beckoned, making the "come here" gesture deep inside her, and she pushed against his quickly moving tongue. She muffled a shriek, clamping her hand across her mouth. Her body stiffened, sweat beading along her forehead and down her throat, even as chilly as it was.

She barely noticed when he moved away from her, so absorbed was she in the sparks and jolts of her orgasm. She trembled, enjoying each burst of heat across her stomach, each clench in the muscles of her groin. She teetered on the very cusp of another orgasm as he pulled his fingers out of her wet depths. Mandu heard the crinkle of a plastic wrapper and looked up to see him remove a condom from its foil packaging.

"Came prepared?" That was good; she was on the pill, but that wouldn't prevent anything else.

"You came. I was prepared," Mitch said. "Doc insisted we all take a handful before we went on leave." He shrugged as if he expected her to believe that. He unzipped his jeans and pushed them down around his thighs. His cock sprang free, thick and heavy.

"And you weren't intending—"

"To get amazingly lucky in a strip club? No, I leave that sort of thing to Conman. But I'm not planning on saying no when it's offered." He gazed at her and Mandu realized what a disheveled mess she must be, her costume half off, her panties hanging on her shoe. "Unless you've changed your mind?"

"Not a chance in hell, Airman."

"Thank God." His relief was palpable. He finished unrolling the condom down his length. "I don't know if I'd survive if you turned me away now."

Mandu opened her arms to him and he tucked himself into

her embrace, his cock seeking her warm depths. She tasted herself on his mouth, kissed him again, licking at his lips. She tipped her hips, lifting her ass up to get a better angle. Mitch found her opening and slid in with a sigh. He waited there, his eyes closed.

She clenched her muscles, pulling him further in. Her arms tightened around him and she squirmed, impaled on his cock, encouraging him to move, and finally he did. He fucked her, hard, driving into her, then pulled almost entirely out, a long, slow slide. Then in again, driving her thighs into the generator, the base of his cock slamming into her clit. He ground his hips against hers, then that fierce, possessive lunge again. As if he couldn't bear to leave her.

"Sweet," he murmured in her ear, "Mandu, you're so sweet, so wet." He thrust again, and then again, desperately pumping into her. He bit down on her collarbone, sharp and heated. She felt the throb of his orgasm, the shuddering of his cock deep within her and she twisted again, rubbing her clit against him, forcing it, harder. *Oh, there, just there.* A moment more and she cried out, a quick exclamation, lost in the sounds as the generator kicked on again under them.

"You got a letter here, Mandy," Tony called out as she walked into work. December was a slow month; she'd only worked two days this past week, and this upcoming week wasn't looking any better for her wages.

Mandu didn't bother to correct him on her name. She was already looking for another job. Tony'd cut her hours first and the most. Other girls on the staff were still pulling in at least twenty-five each week. She was lucky if she'd get seventeen. She snatched her envelope away from him, all the while dodging Tony's wandering hands with the ease of much practice.

Inside were a plane ticket and a scrawled note.

Hey Impatient,

I ran into your brother at the exchange. I bought him a beer and we talked a bit. Why don't you come home for Christmas? I know your brother would love to see you. You can call me if you want; Billy's not the only one who wants to see you again.

Merry Christmas,
Alleycat

P.S. It's me, Mitch. My wingman gave me this flight name just after we left Nevada. It could be worse, though. Peterson threatened to call me Snake for a while. Ugh.

HOME

Michelle Augello-Page

I touch the face of the computer screen; his image is so close, so close that for a second, he doesn't seem so far away. How far away again is Afghanistan? I remind myself that it's 7,500 miles, a fifteen-hour flight. He's almost half a day ahead, in another world. He says he is going on another mission tomorrow. His smile is strained; he looks tired. He says, "Don't worry."

I nod, try to smile, try to be strong. He leans forward, searching my face.

"I'm coming home soon, baby."

"I know," I say, blinking back tears.

"And when I do, you know the first thing I am going to do?"

"What?"

"I am going to hug you so tight you'll think I won't ever let go. And then I'm going to look into your sweet brown eyes and kiss you, and once I get you home, we won't leave that bed for days, if you know what I'm saying."

He laughs and I smile, feeling the knot in my chest loosen

a little bit. He continues talking softly, seductively, as if whispering a secret, words of desire. His voice is hypnotic, rising and falling, turning me on with visions and images. A sharp inhale, a deep exhale, the thrill of excitement, our feverish breath.

"And all you'll be wearing is a pair of high heels. A pair of shiny black fuck-me pumps, and not much else. When I get home, I'm going to buy you a sexy red corset, candy-apple red, with a matching thong, and we won't even come up for air, we've got so much catching up to do. When I get home, I'm going to love you right proper, like a husband should. Understand me?"

"Yes."

"Yes what?"

"Yes, sir," I say shyly, sitting up a little straighter.

"That's better."

He clears his throat and quickly glances at his watch.

"Now stand up so I can see all of you. I need to go soon, but I want to see you before we get offline."

Even though we try to talk on the video cam once a week, and I always wear sexy things under my robe, we usually just talk. Sometimes other officers are around, and he wouldn't take the chance to expose either one of us. But every once in a while, when the coast is clear, he gives me this intimacy.

I stand up and move slightly away from the computer. I let the robe fall to the ground and reveal myself to him.

I look at the screen and can tell that he's unzipping his pants. I feel a hot surge inside, thinking about him touching himself while looking at me. I slowly turn around, feeling suddenly stronger, sexier. The air is cool against my skin. I run my hands along the curve of my waist and hips, down my legs until I touch the tips of my toes. I arch my back so that my butt points up in the air and lightly smack my ass. My golden brown hair brushes the ground.

"You're so pretty," he says.

Eyeing the screen, I smile, seeing his reaction, his thick hard cock pushing through his hand, being caressed and pulled in a rhythmic, rocking movement. How I wish he was here and that his hand was my hand. How I wish he was here so that I could please him, so he could take his pleasure from me.

I touch my breasts; my nipples are hard between my fingers. I cup my breasts with my hands, sweet ripe fruit aching to be tasted. I squeeze the soft, firm flesh and moan, thinking of him licking and sucking my nipples, teasing me with his teeth and tongue. He watches me with intent. His hand doesn't stop. His penis is thick and solid, fully erect, swollen with anticipation and yearning.

"Touch yourself," he says. "I want to see you." His voice is a deep rasp. He doesn't take his eyes off me.

"Yes, sir," I say, moving the chair and sitting on the edge of it. My toes are a flash of color as I curve my ankles around the sides of the chair, forcing me to spread my legs open to him.

I press my hand against the soft fold of my vagina, gently feeling the smooth skin. The excitement stirring between my thighs is torture. I want his long, thick cock taking me. I want his fingers and hands and mouth all over me. I want to press against his body, to feel his skin, naked and hot, yielding. I want him to hold me, to explore me, to discover me. I want to sleep in his waking dreams, to awaken at his touch. I am sticky, wet with desire. I want him so much. I want him here.

"I need you," I say, "I need to feel you inside me."

He moans and I bite my lip, touching my clitoris, finger-painting the nub, the heart sticky sweet with lust, honeyed nectar. I lick my lips and close my eyes, my climax rising, beginning to peak and flush, blooming with the warmth of my desire. I am watching him, watching me.

He breathes in deeply and sharply. Tension and relief play across his face as he comes rapidly, ejaculating his release with a deep sigh.

"I'm sorry that was so quick," he says, cleaning himself up. "It's been a while." He laughs. "Did you come?"

"A little bit," I say, honestly.

"After we get offline, I want you to come really hard, thinking of how good it's going to be when I come home."

"Yes, sir." I smile.

"You know," he says, "I'm a lucky man to have you. Not everyone over here has someone like you, as beautiful and sweet and sexy as you."

I blush, so thankful to have this amazing man hold my heart. He always knows what to say to make me feel like the most special woman in the world.

"And that's what keeps me going over here, day in and day out, because even though I love my country, and I have a job to do here, I'm in hell. And you are my heaven, understand me?"

I nod, so grateful for his love I suddenly feel overwhelmed with emotion. I laugh as tears drop from my eyelashes.

"Don't you ever worry that I'm not coming home. I know I'm coming home, because I'm coming home to you."

I take a deep breath. I say, "I love you."

"I love you too."

This is how we end our conversations; we never say *good-bye*. His eyes are sad, but he flashes me a brilliant smile. He says he loves me one more time, and the screen goes blank. I continue to sit on the chair, not wanting to break the spell. My joy turns silent, heavy with sadness. A moment ago, his voice filled the room. Now the room is empty and quiet. I feel so alone.

This is always the worst part, ending the conversation and not knowing when I will speak to him again. *If I will ever...* I think, then push the thought far from my mind. For the first few months of his deployment, I was a mess. I missed him so much, if there was a way I could have folded myself into one of my care packages to him, I would have.

Each day I mark the calendar with an X, marking this first year without him, my husband, my love. I go to work, I go out with friends. I eat, sleep, breathe. I am here, still, knowing that he is in a world I could barely imagine, a world of instability and chaos, a world where some soldiers die in the line of duty and never come home. Each day I mark the passage of time and pray for his safe return.

It's the little things that get to me. Seeing couples walking hand in hand, kissing, laughing, doing stupid things like shopping for groceries. Meeting someone new and telling them I'm married, then seeing their faces change into the inevitable shocked "oh" when they discover my husband is in Afghanistan. Watching the news, anything to do with the Middle East has me glued to the television, the panic in my head thinking, *Is he okay? Is he safe?* Waiting days for a phone call.

And even though I knew what I signed on for when we married, I wasn't prepared for the void that was created when he was actually deployed and our relationship depended on phone calls, emails, and care packages. Seeing each other over the video camera is a special treat because computer access isn't always guaranteed. But it also makes me miss him more than ever.

I lie across the bed and close my eyes. I try to remember how he looked. Tired, a little thin. Excited to see me. Happy that I put on one of the outfits under my robe. He called me his little tease, his sweet girl, his sexy woman. He wants me to continue where we left off, but I don't want to touch myself. I want him to touch me. I want him to walk through the door and take me, the way he used to.

The way he will, I think, opening my robe, *when he comes home...* in his crisp dress blues with the shiny buttons, matched by the shining sloe black of his shoes. I love how he looks in full uniform, so strong and masculine, heroic. His body is toned and fit, and the uniform accentuates his broad shoulders and long legs. Every step he takes is purposeful, self-assured, confident. His smile could light a room.

I imagine him home. I kneel before him, struck by his stature, and slowly undress him. First his shoes, then his socks. I would wash his feet with my tears and dry them with my hair. I want to kiss his ankles, his toes, the arch and ball of each foot; I want to kiss the places he touches the ground.

Working my way upward, I unfasten his belt, pull it through the loop and offer it to him. He smiles and gently swats my ass with the leather strap. We laugh and I remove his pants, then his jacket, shirt and tie. I look into his eyes, no longer laughing, as he loops the belt around my waist, pulling me toward him so he can kiss me. His tongue dances across my lips, in my mouth, and I feel the hardness of his erection pressing hot against my body.

He drops the belt and touches my breasts with his strong, capable hands. My nipples harden, begging to be kissed, pinched, sucked. I want him so much. He wants to take his time. He's teasing me, running his fingers lightly over my skin. I giggle and laugh, I'm so ticklish I jump. He touches me harder and a moan escapes from somewhere inside me. I am light-headed, filled with want.

"I want you to please me," he says.

It is a command. He knows I love it when he takes control. The familiar response reaches my lips as a flush of heat rushes across my body.

"Yes, sir."

I am eager to obey and fall into place in front of him. I take

his penis into my mouth, admiring the length and thickness of
it. I suck him like a piece of hard candy, explore his tight skin
with my lips and tongue. I feel his hands on my head, grasping
my hair, rocking me back and forth as his cock glides in and out
of my mouth. The head is glistening, pushing deeply through my
lips, and I am ravenous, hungry with desire. I am tasting him,
feeling his smooth hardness inside my mouth. He is a delicacy,
an erotic feast. I am worshipping his cock, and he is breathing
harder, faster, and then he stops, pulling me upward tenderly
by my hair.

We are face-to-face, eye-to-eye, so close I feel his breath on
my lips. He kisses me, lavishing me with his lustful mouth. His
lips touch my cheeks, my eyes, my forehead. He is reading me
with his hands, memorizing the features of my face, touching
me the way the blind see. He picks me up and lays me across
the bed, the altar of desire, and leaves no part of my body
untouched. He sucks and bites my flesh, licking and savoring
the taste of me, then dresses my naked body with butterfly
kisses so soft I tremble.

He holds me tightly in a full embrace. He is here, here! I cling
to him, afraid that if I let go for a second he might disappear.
His eyes are flecked with gold and brown, the center is dark
with desire. He is flushed, feverish. I run my hands along his
smooth, strong back, letting my fingernails gently scratch the
surface of his skin. My body is on fire. I feel the heat between
my legs rising.

"I need you," I say. "Please, sir."

Hearing my own voice beg him makes me even hotter. My
heart is beating wildly. I am dripping wet and open with longing.
I am breathless; I can barely speak.

I whisper, "I need to feel you inside me."

He crushes my body with his. He is above me on his knees;

his cock is impatient, pushing lightly against my pussy. I open my legs wider, wrapping myself around him. He pulls my wrists above my head, holding my hands, our fingers entwined. His skin is pressed against my skin, his breath is my breath. He enters me slowly. He is torturing me. I feel the thrill of his cock pushing into my moist cunt.

It feels so good that I cry out loudly. His dick is electric, hard and thick, driving inside me with masterful control. He moves slowly, deliberately, lingering with delight as he watches my face respond to his touch. My eyes are half-closed, lips open, sighing and moaning a song of ecstasy. He thrusts inside me and waves of pleasure take me further and further into bliss.

We move together as one, curling our sweetness into a ball, basking in the wonder, in the delight of our lovemaking. I no longer know where my body ends and his begins.

He falls into me and we rest together for a moment, panting. His excitement is at a fevered pitch. He pulls me on top of him and a rush of cool air surrounds us. His cock is swollen and rigid, inexhaustible. He rests inside me, fitting into me like a puzzle piece, perfectly. He spanks my ass, demanding my voice to cry out again as each slap leaves a lingering sting and a ripple of pleasure through my body.

Placing his hands on my tingling butt cheeks, he lifts me up and down on his cock furiously. I am riding his torrential current; his balls slap my ass. My clitoris is being rubbed in just the right way as he rocks me up and down, back and forth. He is controlling my every movement as I twist with pleasure. I throw my head back as I feel him suddenly grow harder. He tells me to come, and just hearing his command is enough to put me over the edge.

I feel his throbbing cock stroking me deeply as he takes me harder, fucking me fast with hot, hot fury. I am shivering, swelling with pleasure, rising and falling, holding on to him in a tight embrace. Our bodies are slick, scorched with heat and beads of sweat. I shudder and scream in a violent sob of climax so deep and complete I shake, breaking into joy. He roars and releases, coming deep inside me, flooding me with hot fluid. We are body, arms and legs and skin, flushed with fevered brightness. We are twin flames, vibrating rays of sun, light encircled with love. He is my husband, my lover, the prayer on my lips. Light-years away, he sends a wish across the desert. He whispers into the wind, sending a kiss across the luminous sky, saying my name. He calls me home.

FOR BETTER
OR WORSE

Kristina Wright

It wasn't exactly the honeymoon cruise I had hoped for. For one thing, La Maddalena (known as La Madd to sailors everywhere) wasn't much of a honeymoon destination by myself. It was a lovely little village, and even the base wasn't as bad as some I'd seen in Europe, but my heart wasn't in exploring the piazzas or basking in the sun on a rocky beach. My heart was on a Navy destroyer making boxes in the ocean somewhere offshore.

Joe was deployed. I was deployed. We are the modern navy couple. The catch was we were on different ships in the same battle group. We were hitting all the same ports—Palma, Marseilles, Cartegena, now La Madd and next Naples. We could walk the same streets, hit the same tourist spots, drink in the same bars and we would never cross paths. It would have been funny if it wasn't so frustrating.

Three months. We'd hit the halfway mark and it was all downhill from here. That thought should have comforted me.

But hot tears pricked my eyes as I maneuvered the yellow scooter I'd rented through the streets crowded with European tourists, American sailors and locals. I missed Joe. And I was lonely. Fucking lonely.

I brought the scooter to a jolting halt near a corner café, recognizing the name Joe had told me about. That was one of the benefits—hell, the *only* benefit—of him always being a couple of days ahead of me. He could tell me which spots to hit if I bothered to get off the ship. The tiny café with dingy orange shutters didn't look like much, but I was starving. I rubbed at my watery eyes as I parked the scooter and went inside.

The place smelled of spices and earth and wine and that smell unique to an island that was part ocean, part sunshine, part history. It smelled like heaven. I made eye contact with the pretty young waitress as I took a seat and she nodded in acknowledgment. A boisterous voice from the doorway made me smile.

"Damn, girl, you took off on me!" Marjorie complained as she tucked her six-foot frame into the chair next to me. "I thought you'd gotten abducted by one of those swarthy Italian fellas."

Marjorie pronounced *Italian* as "Eye-talian," and that made me laugh. Petty Officer Second Class Marjorie Janks was a machinist's mate, my liberty buddy and my best friend since boot camp. She was a wide-hipped girl from Millersville, Iowa, with a big mouth and a bigger heart, and she could wield a mechanic's wrench like nobody's business.

"Wouldn't that be a swarthy Sardinian?"

"I don't know. I had watch and missed the geography lesson," Marjorie said. "Eye-talian, Sardinian, Corsican, they're all swarthy!"

I laughed. "Well, I know you'd have my back no matter what."

I wasn't interested in swarthy Italians or swarthy Sardinians or swarthy *anything*. The sad truth was I wished I were back on the ship, doing my job. Staying busy. Everybody wanted to go on liberty—buy some trinkets and postcards for the family back home, dip their toes in the ocean instead of only seeing it from a steel deck, drink the night away before falling into a bed with a mattress that was more than a quarter inch thick. Not me. I just wanted this deployment *over*. But I'd promised Joe I would at least get off the ship this port visit.

"Go do something," he'd urged me in his email last night. "Go explore. La Madd is kind of pretty. It'll be fun."

His destroyer had pulled in a week ago—and pulled out three days before the carrier, my ship, pulled in. It had been like that for three months—us shadowing each other across the Med, so close but not close enough. With only emails and the occasional phone call to sustain us, it seemed like Joe was always just out of sight. He might as well have been at home back in Norfolk, in the apartment we had shared for our brief, whirlwind engagement.

The navy was a calling for both of us and we both planned to reenlist. We had wanted to get married before the deployment with the hopes that when Joe came up for orders he'd be able to convince his detailer to keep him in Norfolk. But there had been no time for a honeymoon. Just a couple nights at a bed-and-breakfast in Williamsburg and then it was time to muster for deployment.

"Aw, Em, you're killing me with those sad little faces of yours," Marjorie said.

I tried to smile, knowing I looked as morose as I felt. If not for Marjorie, I would have lost it a lot more often in the past three months than I was willing to admit. "We need to find you a swarthy Italian girl, Marj."

Marjorie's laugh was as big and full of life as she was. "Hell, you know I'm playing the field. I'll settle down with Ms. Right when I get out of the navy. Not interested in long-distance anything, and this"—she gestured at me—"this mopey love-sickness has totally turned me off to finding love in the navy."

"You can't help when or how you fall in love. I should know."

The dark-haired waitress brought a bottle of wine with our lunch and I savored the rich red. The pasta was simple but fresh and tossed with olive oil, mussels, crushed tomato and basil. Perfect. *Almost.*

"If you don't snap out of it, I'm going to tell Joe," Marjorie warned.

That got a laugh. It was an ongoing joke between us since the deployment had begun. Marjorie was my keeper and would report to Joe if I didn't at least pretend I was doing okay. "I wonder how he is?"

"That man of yours is missing you just as much as you're missing him." Marjorie waved her fork in the air. "And soon you'll be fuckin' like bunnies and you will have forgotten all about this deployment."

"I hope you're right." I tucked my hair behind my ears. I had been letting it grow out because Joe liked it long, but I was tired of having to pin it up for work. "This sucks. No offense."

"No offense taken."

A burst of laughter outside the open window startled me out of my gloomy thoughts. "That sounded just like Joe."

Marjorie shook her head. "Poor lovesick girl. Next you'll be seeing apparitions of him."

"No, seriously. That sounded just like him."

"Swarthy Eye-talian alert," Marjorie muttered.

I thought she was referring to the laugh we heard, but then I saw the barrel-chested older man approaching our table.

"Excuse me? I am Roberto, I own Il Giallo del Sole," he said in accented English.

I smiled. "You have a lovely café."

He returned the smile with a flash of white teeth and nodded. "Thank you, miss. I have something for you."

I stared at the small manila envelope he handed me. "What's this?"

He spread his arms in an expansive shrug. "A man came in. Said to give it to you. Excuse me."

Before I could ask what man, Roberto left to greet a large group of what sounded like German tourists. I turned the envelope over in my hands, recognizing the handwriting immediately.

"Joe!"

"Well, open it, will you," Marjorie said. "The suspense is killing me."

I ran my finger along the sealed edge of the envelope and dumped the contents on the table. A postcard of one of the old hotels that dotted La Madd and a printout of a one-night reservation for a room at Il Sicirao.

"Ooh, a mystery!"

Ignoring Marjorie, I read the note in Joe's messy handwriting: *Thought you could use a night away from the ship. I wanted to stay here with you. Tonight is for you to enjoy. Three more months, sweetheart.*

The tears were flowing then. I couldn't stop them. Marjorie snatched the postcard from me and read Joe's note.

"Aw, that's a sweet boy you have, Emily." She patted my hand awkwardly. "Come on. Let's hit the beach and I'll drop you at the hotel before I head back to the ship."

"I can't take this," I sniffled.

"Hang in there." Marjorie gave me a stern look. "You'll see him soon!"

I wanted to say it felt like forever, but I didn't. I let Marjorie coax me out into the sunshine for a drive to the beach. Killing time. I was just killing time.

"Three months, Joe," I whispered, leaving the café behind.

The beach was gorgeous, the rocky coastline dotted with terra-cotta roofs and the ocean a beautiful shade of blue. I took Marjorie's advice as best I could and stopped thinking about the long weeks stretched out in front of me. I basked in the sun and the smell of the ocean, somehow different here on La Maddalena than it was from the ship.

By the time we were asking directions to the hotel from one of the fishermen hauling his catch from the pier, I was starting to feel more like myself. I tried to convince Marjorie to stay with me since we had to have a liberty buddy, but she emphatically shook her head.

"You need a night alone and there's an equally decrepit hotel down the street. I can crash there. Kinda glad your man did this for you because I'm sick to death of the ship's berthing," she said. "I'll see you in the morning." With that, she motored off on her scooter and left me in front of Il Sicirao.

I couldn't say I was disappointed. While I hadn't been in a hurry to hit any of the ports on this deployment and preferred the familiarity and routine of the ship to make the days go by, I was kind of excited to contemplate a night in a hotel room by myself.

Il Sicirao was four stories and didn't have an elevator, so I wasn't expecting much from the accommodations. It didn't matter. I hadn't been truly alone in three months and it wouldn't take a lot to make me happy—a bed, a bath, some peace and quiet. I checked in at the front desk and the gray-haired woman handed me an old-fashioned room key along with a brown paper bag.

"Your husband, he thought you might need some things."

I blinked quickly to keep from crying again. "Thank you, thank you," I said, though I was really talking to Joe.

My room was on the top floor and was more than I could've hoped for. Small by American standards, it was still lovely. The bed was enormous and covered in soft linens and pillows and the bathroom was modernized, the claw-foot bathtub quaint and inviting. French doors looked out over the rust-colored rooftops of La Madd, and though I was a mile or so inland, I could still smell the ocean. It was perfect. *Almost.*

I distracted myself by looking through the bag Joe had prepared for me. All the necessities were there. Toothbrush, toothpaste, hairbrush, my favorite moisturizer and lip balm and...a pair of panties. Leave it to Joe to know I'd want fresh underwear in the morning.

It wasn't even dark yet, but the lure of that big European bed was more than I could resist. I kicked off my sneakers and stretched out, figuring I would sleep for a couple of hours and then get some dinner. I'd barely had time to contemplate why the pillows smelled like Joe's aftershave before sleep claimed me and I was dreaming about him.

"Hey baby," Joe said in my dream. "I've missed you."

I sighed and turned my head, nuzzling his shoulder. It felt so real. The sounds of voices and laughter in the street below. The smell of Joe's aftershave mingling with the scent of the ocean and freshly laundered sheets. The feel of his calloused fingers caressing my shoulder. So...real. *Too* real. One minute I was asleep, the next my eyes were wide open and I was staring up at Joe in the lamplight.

"Sleepyhead," he said affectionately, tucking my hair behind my ear as I sat up.

"What? Joe! Oh my god." I was laughing and crying at the same time, making a full-on spectacle of myself. "Why didn't you tell me?"

Joe laughed. "Because I wanted to surprise you."

I couldn't catch my breath or stop staring at him. He looked so *good*. His blond hair was freshly cut and his year-round tan was set off by the white polo shirt and khakis that he wore. I realized I was running my hands up and down his muscular forearms, but I couldn't stop. I needed to touch him. Needed to be close to him. Closer than this.

"How?" I asked breathlessly, pulling him closer and burying my face in his neck.

"I told them I wanted to reenlist on deployment and that I wanted my wife to be there for it and this is what Chief came up with. The helo picked me up when they brought mail over. We get tonight and the reenlistment ceremony is in the morning." Joe pressed a kiss to the top of my head. "Then I'm hitching a ride on your boat for a couple of days and the helo will take me back."

One night. No way in hell we were going to do anything on the ship, so we had one night.

"It's only one night," he said, as if reading my mind, "but it's better than nothing."

"One night in six months." I hooked a leg over his thigh, his erection a noticeable presence. "I guess we'd better make it count."

He didn't say anything. He didn't have to. His mouth covered mine and absorbed my moan. I felt like every nerve ending in my body was tingling with the familiarity of his touch after having gone so long without it. He ran his hand down my arm to the curve of my hip and back up to my breast, cupping it gently and thumbing my nipple until it peaked under his touch. I whimpered, touching him, pulling him closer, pulling at his shirt, struggling to get his belt unfastened.

He pulled away, holding me at arm's length, staring into my eyes while both of us panted. "We have all night," he said. "But I don't think I can wait to be inside you."

I reached for him, resuming my work on his belt. "So hurry up and help me get your pants off!"

He laughed, that familiar happy-go-lucky laugh that had been one of the many reasons I'd fallen in love with him. Everything would be all right with Joe. Everything.

He let me work his belt free while he got my pants unfastened. "It would be easier if we each got our own clothes off."

"But not as much fun," I said with a wicked grin as I got his khakis open and reached inside to palm his erection over his underwear.

He groaned. "Damn, baby. I've jerked off twice a day every day for a week just so I could make this last, but I don't think it was enough. Three months is too long to go without you."

I thrilled to hear how excited he was for me. I tumbled him back on the bed, straddling his waist and rubbing against him like a cat in heat. "We have all night, remember? We can go again and again and again, all night long."

He anchored his hands on my hips and thrust up against me. "I like the sound of that, though I'm not sure I can keep up with you."

"You can try."

He bolted upright, arm around my waist, and flipped me over on my back so that I was pinned beneath his weight. "I intend to," he said.

They say absence makes the heart grow fonder, but they

don't tell you what it does to the rest of your body. My skin felt feverish and hypersensitive under his gentle touch. He pushed my shirt up and reached under me to release the clasp on my plain white bra.

"I would've worn sexier underwear if I'd known I was going to see you," I said by way of an apology.

"Honey, you could be wearing a burlap sack and I'd think you were the sexiest woman in the world." To prove the truth of his words, he lowered his mouth to my breast, tonguing each nipple until they were hard, sensitive peaks aching for rougher treatment.

I gasped, pressing my thighs together and writhing on the bed. I could feel the moisture gathering between my thighs, soaking through my panties and pants. Joe stripped off the remainder of my clothes, inhaling deeply as he knelt between my legs.

"Oh god, how I've missed your smell," he said. "I don't even have to touch you—I can see how wet you are."

I squirmed under his steady gaze, aroused and embarrassed and so in love I thought my heart would burst out of my chest. "I need you," I whispered. "Now."

He moved as if to go down on me and I shook my head. "No. Later. Right now, I just want to feel you inside me. Please, Joe. I've *missed* you."

"Whatever you want, baby," he said, stripping his shirt over his head. "Tonight is for you."

That's what his note had said, only I hadn't had any idea what he meant. I waited impatiently for him to finish undressing, to fling his clothes away so that it was just him and me naked in this big bed. I took a deep breath, not realizing I'd been holding it until air filled my lungs. At that moment, Joe plunged into me in one long stroke, his cock filling the deep ache inside me.

I cried out—I hadn't intended to, I just couldn't help myself. The sudden sensation of fullness was almost too much to bear. *Almost.* I wrapped my arms and legs around him, clinging to him, pulling him deeper into me. I whimpered and gasped against the hard muscle of his shoulder, nipping at the corded tendons in his neck and being rewarded with another long, driving stroke.

"God, baby, I don't think I'll last very long," he said through gritted teeth. "You feel so damn good."

I laughed. "Really? Are you going to come already?"

"I might," he said, the words sounding like a growl in his throat.

I tightened my pussy around his erection and rotated my hips, drunk with feminine power. "Not before I do," I said. "Tonight is for me, remember?"

"Then you'd better hurry, sweetheart."

He didn't have to tell me twice. Despite my teasing, I was no more in control of my body's response than Joe was, and I hadn't been masturbating like a fiend in preparation for this night.

My gyrations served to press my swollen clit against his pubic bone and every twist of my hips was bringing me closer to the edge. I tensed against him, my legs wrapped high around his broad back, my hips angled up so that every shallow thrust bumped my G-spot. I knew his short, quick thrusts were to help him last, but they were having the opposite effect on me. I let him do the work, my mouth pressed to his neck to stifle another scream as my orgasm washed over me in a steady wave of sensation. My arousal soaked the sheets beneath me and I clung to him, urging him on, making my orgasm last and last.

Finally, he pushed deep into me and went still, his cock pulsing in release. I tightened my muscles around him as he thrust again and moaned as loud as I had. He dropped his head to the pillow and laughed.

"I lasted longer than I expected. I thought I was going to go off just walking up the stairs."

"Probably a good thing you didn't," I said. "You'd be confined to the ship and I'd be here all alone. I have missed you so much!"

He raised up to look at me, his expression suddenly serious. "If I reenlist tomorrow, there will be more deployments."

"I know. And if I reenlist next year, I'll have more deployments, too."

"You're okay with that?"

I hesitated. Was I okay with it? I traced a finger along the line of his square jaw, feeling just the hint of stubble. I shook my head. "I will *never* be okay with being apart from you for a day or a week or a month or six months, but this is the career you chose. And the career I chose."

He nodded. "It's going to be hell."

"I'm in it for the long haul," I promised. "For better or worse, in peacetime or wartime, sea duty or shore duty."

"Me, too."

I remembered something. "Oh hell, I don't have a change of clothes, much less my uniform, and you're reenlisting in the morning?"

He tucked a stray wisp of hair behind my ear and kissed my nose. "Marjorie has been my partner in crime. How do you think Roberto at the restaurant knew who you were? She made sure to smuggle everything you need off the ship and she'll bring it by in the morning. The paper bag was just for tonight."

I shook my head in wonder, at both his sneakiness and the beginnings of his erection that was making itself known against my thigh. "You are something else."

"I'm *yours*. That's all I want to be."

I rubbed my hands in slow circles across his sweat-slick back, shifting my hips to accommodate his renewed arousal. "I still can't believe you're here."

He lowered his head until his lips brushed mine. "I have all night to prove it."

ABOUT THE AUTHORS

MICHELLE AUGELLO-PAGE (michelleaugellopage.word-press.com) writes erotica, poetry and gothic fiction. Her work has appeared in art exhibitions, online journals, print publications and anthologies. She is also a teacher and a mother and lives in New York. Recent erotica was published in *Fairy Tale Lust* and *Lustfully Ever After*.

ELIZABETH L. BROOKS (everyworldneedslove.blogspot.com) taught herself to read at the age of three and started writing stories when she was five, though it took her a little longer to work up to erotica. She writes mostly romance, sci-fi and fantasy.

J.K. COI writes contemporary and paranormal romance and urban fantasy. She lives in Ontario, Canada, with her husband, son and a feisty black cat. She spends her days in the litigious world of insurance law and her nights writing dark, sexy characters who leap off the page and into readers' hearts.

Multi-published author **CHRISTINE D'ABO** loves exploring the human condition through a romantic lens. She takes her characters on fantastical journeys that change their hearts and expand their minds. When she's not writing, she can be found chasing after her children, dogs or husband.

DELILAH DEVLIN (DelilahDevlin.com) is an award-winning author with a rapidly expanding reputation for writing deliciously edgy stories with complex characters. Whether creating dark, erotically charged paranormal worlds or richly descriptive Westerns that ring with authenticity, Delilah Devlin "pens in uncharted territory that will leave the readers breathless and hungering for more...."

LUCY FELTHOUSE (lucyfelthouse.co.uk) studied creative writing at university. Whilst there, she was dared to write an erotic story. It went down a storm and she's never looked back. Lucy has had stories published by Cleis Press, Constable and Robinson, Noble Romance, Ravenous Romance, Summerhouse Publishing, Sweetmeats Press and Xcite Books.

SHANNA GERMAIN claims the titles of leximaven, she-devil, vorpal blonde and Schrödinger's brat. Her work has appeared in places like *Best American Erotica*, *Best Erotic Romance*, *Best Gay Romance*, *Best Lesbian Erotica* and *Dream Lover*. Visit her wild world of words at shannagermain.com.

SACCHI GREEN's stories have appeared in a hip-high stack of publications with erotically inspirational covers, and she's also edited or co-edited seven volumes of erotica, including *Girl Crazy*, *Lesbian Cowboys* (winner of the 2010 Lambda Literary

Award for lesbian erotica), *Lesbian Lust* and *Lesbian Cops*, all from Cleis Press.

ERICKA HIATT lives and writes in the Silicon Valley. She has published several technical works, as well as a number of short stories. Her first erotic story appeared in *Dream Lover: Paranormal Tales of Erotic Romance*.

CAT JOHNSON writes contemporary military and western erotic romance for Kensington and Samhain Publishing. She's known for her creative research and marketing techniques. Consequently, some of her closest friends/book consultants wear combat boots for a living and she owns an entire collection of camouflage for book signings.

MERCY LOOMIS (mercyloomis.com) graduated from college one class short of an accidental certificate in folklore. She has a BA in psychology, but don't hold that against her. Her favorite pastimes include road trips and studying ancient history.

KELLY MAHER loves that she can dream up romantic and erotic stories to share with the world while also working with such literature in her day life as a librarian. Previous work has been published with Black Lace and Ellora's Cave. She lives in the Washington, DC area.

After years of living in England and Israel, **CATHERINE PAULSSEN** now enjoys the magic and excitement of her new hometown, Berlin. She loves old Hollywood movies, Motown music, and cooking for friends and family. During the day, she works as a freelancer; every spare minute is dedicated to writing erotica.

After living a checkered past, and despite an avowed disinterest in domesticity, multi-published author **ANYA RICHARDS** settled in Ontario, Canada, with husband, kids and two cats who plot world domination, one food bowl at a time. To find out more about her writing, drop by Anya's website at anyarichards.com.

Though **CRAIG J. SORENSEN**'s (just-craig.blogspot.com) military career lasted just four years, those times remain a source of inspiration to this day. His erotic stories, dotted with tales of sexy military life, have been published internationally in print and electronic media.

CHARLOTTE STEIN (themightycharlottestein.blogspot.com) has published a number of stories in various erotic anthologies, including *Sexy Little Numbers*. She is also the author of the short story collection *The Things That Make Me Give In* and a novella, *Waiting In Vain*.

LYNN TOWNSEND (paidbytheweird.blogspot.com) is a displaced Yankee, a mother, a writer, a dreamer and the proud owner of a small black hole residing under her desk. Her short stories are included in the anthologies *Steamlust*, *Lustfully Every After* and *Shifting Steam*.

CONNIE WILKINS began by writing fantasy and science fiction, but she's often seduced by the erotic side of the force, with stories in a number of very sexy anthologies. On the speculative fiction front she's the editor of *Time Well Bent: Queer Alternative History* and co-editor (with Steve Berman) of *Heiresses of Russ 2012: The Year's Best Lesbian Speculative Fiction*, both from Lethe Press.

ABOUT
THE EDITOR

Described by The Romance Reader as "a budding force to be reckoned with," **KRISTINA WRIGHT** (kristinawright.com) had no idea what to expect from military life when she married an enlisted sailor after a whirlwind long-distance courtship just three months before the first Gulf War. Military life may not be for everyone, but it's been one hell of a ride for her! In the twenty-two years since they said "I do," her husband James has worked his way up the ranks to lieutenant commander and she has become an award-winning author whose erotic fiction has appeared in over one hundred anthologies. They have lived in three states, endured seven deployments (two while he was assigned to navy special warfare) and countless months of training exercises and counternarcotics operations. Their first son was born in 2009 while James was on an eight-month deployment to the Middle East, but he was lucky enough to be stateside for the birth of their second son in 2011.

Inspired by her South Florida roots and tales of drug

running and espionage, Kristina's first novel received the
Golden Heart Award for Romantic Suspense from Romance
Writers of America. She has edited the Cleis Press anthologies
Fairy Tale Lust: Erotic Fantasies for Women; *Dream Lover:
Paranormal Tales of Erotic Romance*; *Steamlust: Steampunk
Erotic Romance*; the *Best Erotic Romance* series and *Lustfully
Ever After: Fairy Tale Erotic Romance*. Her first anthology,
Fairy Tale Lust, was nominated for a Reviewers' Choice
Award by *RT Book Reviews* and was a featured alternate of
the Doubleday Book Club. Her work has also been featured
in the nonfiction guide *The Many Joys of Sex Toys* and maga-
zines and e-zines such as Clean Sheets, Good Vibes Magazine,
*Libida, The Fiction Writer, The Literary Times, Scarlet Letters,
The Sun* and *The Quill*. Her nonfiction essay "The Last Letter"
is included in the epistolary anthology *P.S. What I Didn't
Say: Unsent Letters to Our Female Friends*. She is a member
of Romance Writers of America as well as the RWA special
interest chapters Passionate Ink and Fantasy, Futuristic and
Paranormal. She is a book reviewer for the Erotica Readers and
Writers Association (erotica-readers.com) and a regular blogger
at Oh Get a Grip! (ohgetagrip.blogspot.com) and Good Vibrations Magazine (magazine.goodvibes.com). She holds degrees
in English and humanities and has taught English composi-
tion and world mythology at the community college level. She
currently lives with her family in Hampton Roads, Virginia,
home to the legendary SEAL Team Six and the largest naval
base in the world.

More from Kristina Wright

Best Erotic Romance
Edited by Kristina Wright

This year's collection is the debut of a new series!
"Kristina is a phenomenal writer...she has the enviable
ability to tell a story and simultaneously excite her
readers." —Erotica Readers and Writers Association
ISBN 978-1-57344-751-5 $14.95

Steamlust
Steampunk Erotic Romance
Edited by Kristina Wright

"Turn the page with me and step into
the new worlds...where airships rule
the skies, where romance and intellect
are valued over money and social status,
where lovers boldly discover each other's
bodies, minds and hearts." —from the
foreword by Meljean Brook
ISBN 978-1-57344-721-8 $14.95

Dream Lover
Paranormal Tales of Erotic Romance
Edited by Kristina Wright

Supernaturally sensual and captivating,
the stories in *Dream Lover* will fill you
with a craving that defies the rules of life,
death and gravity. "...A choice of paranormal seduction for every reader. All are
original and entertaining." —*Romantic
Times*
ISBN 978-1-57344-655-6 $14.95

Fairy Tale Lust
Erotic Fantasies for Women
Edited by Kristina Wright

Award-winning novelist and erotica
writer Kristina Wright goes over the
river and through the woods to find the
sexiest fairy tales ever written. "Deliciously sexy action to make your heart
beat faster." —Angela Knight, the *New
York Times* bestselling author of *Guardian*
ISBN 978-1-57344-397-5 $14.95

Lustfully Ever After
Fairy Tale Erotic Romance
Edited by Kristina Wright

Even grown-ups need bedtime stories, and
this delightful collection of fairy tales will
lead you down a magical path into forbidden romance and erotic love. The authors
of *Lustfully Ever After* know your heart's
most wicked and secret desires.
ISBN 978-1-57344-787-4 $14.95

Red Hot Erotic Romance

Obsessed
Erotic Romance for Women
Edited by Rachel Kramer Bussel

These stories sizzle with the kind of obsession that is fueled by our deepest desires, the ones that hold couples together, the ones that haunt us and don't let go. Whether just-blooming passions, rekindled sparks or reinvented relationships, these lovers put the object of their obsession first.
ISBN 978-1-57344-718-8 $14.95

Passion
Erotic Romance for Women
Edited by Rachel Kramer Bussel

Love and sex have always been intimately intertwined—and *Passion* shows just how delicious the possibilities are when they mingle in this sensual collection edited by award-winning author Rachel Kramer Bussel.
ISBN 978-1-57344-415-6 $14.95

Girls Who Bite
Lesbian Vampire Erotica
Edited by Delilah Devlin

Bestselling romance writer Delilah Devlin and her contributors add fresh girl-on-girl blood to the pantheon of the paranormal. The stories in *Girls Who Bite* are varied, unexpected, and soul-scorching.
ISBN 978-1-57344-715-7 $14.95

Irresistible
Erotic Romance for Couples
Edited by Rachel Kramer Bussel

This prolific editor has gathered the most popular fantasies and created a sizzling, no-holds-barred collection of explicit encounters in which couples turn their deepest desires into reality.
978-1-57344-762-1 $14.95

Heat Wave
Hot, Hot, Hot Erotica
Edited by Alison Tyler

What could be sexier or more seductive than bare, sun-warmed skin? Bestselling erotica author Alison Tyler gathers explicit stories of summer sex bursting with the sweet eroticism of swimsuits, sprinklers, and ripe strawberries.
ISBN 978-1-57344-710-2 $15.95

Many More Than Fifty Shades of Erotica

Please, Sir
Erotic Stories of Female Submission
Edited by Rachel Kramer Bussel

If you liked *Fifty Shades of Grey*, you'll love the explosive stories of *Yes, Sir*. These damsels delight in the pleasures of taking risks to be rewarded by the men who know their deepest desires. Find out why nothing is as hot as the power of the words "Please, Sir."
ISBN 978-1-57344-389-0 $14.95

Yes, Sir
Erotic Stories of Female Submission
Edited by Rachel Kramer Bussel

Bound, gagged or spanked—or controlled with just a glance—these lucky women experience the breathtaking thrills of sexual submission. *Yes, Sir* shows that pleasure is best when dispensed by a firm hand.
ISBN 978-1-57344-310-4 $15.95

He's on Top
Erotic Stories of Male Dominance and Female Submission
Edited by Rachel Kramer Bussel

As true tops, the bossy hunks in these stories understand that BDSM is about exulting in power that is freely yielded. These kinky stories celebrate women who know exactly what they want.
ISBN 978-1-57344-270-1 $14.95

Best Bondage Erotica 2012
Edited by Rachel Kramer Bussel

How do you want to be teased, tied and tantalized? Whether you prefer a tough top with shiny handcuffs, the tug of rope on your skin or the sound of your lover's command, Rachel Kramer Bussel serves your needs.
ISBN 978-1-57344-754-6 $15.95

Bottoms Up
Spanking Good Stories
Edited by Rachel Kramer Bussel

As sweet as it is kinky, *Bottoms Up* will propel you to pick up a paddle and share in both pleasure and pain, or perhaps simply turn the other cheek. This torrid tour de force is essential reading.
ISBN 978-1-57344-362-3 $15.95

Read the Very Best in Erotica

Fairy Tale Lust
Erotic Fantasies for Women
Edited by Kristina Wright
Foreword by Angela Knight

Award-winning novelist and top erotica writer Kristina Wright goes over the river and through the woods to find the sexiest fairy tales ever written.
ISBN 978-1-57344-397-5 $14.95

In Sleeping Beauty's Bed
Erotic Fairy Tales
By Mitzi Szereto

"Classic fairy tale characters like Rapunzel, Little Red Riding Hood, Cinderella, and Sleeping Beauty, just to name a few, are brought back to life in Mitzi Szereto's delightful collection of erotica fairy tales."
—Nancy Madore, author of *Enchanted: Erotic Bedtime Stories for Women*
ISBN 978-1-57344-376-8 $16.95

Frenzy
60 Stories of Sudden Sex
Edited by Alison Tyler

"Toss out the roses and box of candies. This isn't a prolonged seduction. This is slammed against the wall in an alleyway sex, and it's all that much hotter for it."
—Erotica Readers & Writers Association
ISBN 978-1-57344-331-9 $14.95

Fast Girls
Erotica for Women
Edited by Rachel Kramer Bussel

Fast Girls celebrates the girl with a reputation, the girl who goes all the way, and the girl who doesn't know how to say "no."
ISBN 978-1-57344-384-5 $14.95

Can't Help the Way That I Feel
Sultry Stories of African American Love, Lust and Fantasy
Edited by Lori Bryant-Woolridge

Some temptations are just too tantalizing to ignore in this collection of delicious stories edited by Emmy award-winning and *Essence* bestselling author Lori Bryant-Woolridge.
ISBN 978-1-57344-386-9 $14.95

Bestselling Erotica for Couples

Sweet Life
Erotic Fantasies for Couples
Edited by Violet Blue

Your ticket to a front row seat for first-time spankings, breathtaking role-playing scenes, sex parties, women who strap it on and men who love to take it, not to mention threesomes of every combination.
ISBN 978-1-57344-133-9 $14.95

Sweet Life 2
Erotic Fantasies for Couples
Edited by Violet Blue

"This is a we-did-it-you-can-too anthology of real couples playing out their fantasies." —Lou Paget, author of *365 Days of Sensational Sex*
ISBN 978-1-57344-167-4 $15.95

Sweet Love
Erotic Fantasies for Couples
Edited by Violet Blue

"If you ever get a chance to try out your number-one fantasies in real life—and I assure you, there will be more than one—say yes. It's well worth it. May this book, its adventurous authors, and the daring and satisfied characters be your guiding inspiration."—Violet Blue
ISBN 978-1-57344-381-4 $14.95

Afternoon Delight
Erotica for Couples
Edited by Alison Tyler

"Alison Tyler evokes a world of heady sensuality where fantasies are fearlessly explored and dreams gloriously realized."
—Barbara Pizio, Executive Editor, *Penthouse Variations*
ISBN 978-1-57344-341-8 $14.95

Three-Way
Erotic Stories
Edited by Alison Tyler

"Three means more of everything. Maybe I'm greedy, but when it comes to sex, I like more. More fingers. More tongues. More limbs. More tangling and wrestling on the mattress."
ISBN 978-1-57344-193-3 $15.95

Love, Lust and Desire

Red Velvet and Absinthe
Paranormal Erotic Romance
Edited by Mitzi Szereto

Explore love and lust with otherworldly partners who, by
their sheer unearthly nature, evoke passion and desire far
beyond that which any normal human being can inspire.
ISBN 978-1-57344-716-4 $14.95

In Sleeping Beauty's Bed
Erotic Fairy Tales
By Mitzi Szereto

"Making their way into the spotlight again,
Rapunzel, Little Red Riding Hood,
Cinderella, and Sleeping Beauty, just to
name a few, are brought back to life in
Mitzi Szereto's delightful collection of
erotic fairy tales."
—Nancy Madore, author of *Enchanted*
ISBN 978-1-57344-367-8 $16.95

Foreign Affairs
Erotic Travel Tales
Edited by Mitzi Szereto

"With vignettes set in such romantic lo-
cales as Dubai, St. Lucia and Brussels, this
is the perfect book to accompany you on
your journeys."
—*Adult Video News*
ISBN 978-1-57344-192-6 $14.95

Pride and Prejudice
Hidden Lusts
By Mitzi Szereto

"If Jane Austen had drunk a great deal of
absinthe and slipped out of her petticoat...
Mitzi Szereto's erotic parody of *Pride and
Prejudice* might well be the result!"
—Susie Bright
978-1-57344-663-1 $15.95

Wicked
Sexy Tales of Legendary Lovers
Edited by Mitzi Szereto

"Funny, sexy, hot, clever, witty, erotic, pro-
vocative, poignant and just plain smart—
this anthology is an embarrassment of
riches. "
—M. J. Rose, author of *The Reincarnationist*
and *The Halo Effect*
ISBN 978-1-57344-206-0 $14.95

Best Erotica Series

"Gets racier every year."—*San Francisco Bay Guardian*

Buy 4 books,
Get 1 *FREE**

Best Women's Erotica 2012
Edited by Violet Blue
ISBN 978-1-57344-755-3 $15.95

Best Women's Erotica 2011
Edited by Violet Blue
ISBN 978-1-57344-423-1 $15.95

Best Women's Erotica 2010
Edited by Violet Blue
ISBN 978-1-57344-373-9 $15.95

Best Bondage Erotica 2012
Edited by Rachel Kramer Bussel
ISBN 978-1-57344-754-6 $15.95

Best Bondage Erotica 2011
Edited by Rachel Kramer Bussel
ISBN 978-1-57344-426-2 $15.95

Best Fetish Erotica
Edited by Cara Bruce
ISBN 978-1-57344-355-5 $15.95

Best Lesbian Erotica 2012
Edited by Kathleen Warnock. Selected and
introduced by Sinclair Sexsmith.
ISBN 978-1-57344-752-2 $15.95

Best Lesbian Erotica 2011
Edited by Kathleen Warnock.
Selected and introduced by Lea DeLaria.
ISBN 978-1-57344-425-5 $15.95

Best Lesbian Erotica 2010
Edited by Kathleen Warnock.
Selected and introduced by BETTY.
ISBN 978-1-57344-375-3 $15.95

Best Gay Erotica 2012
Edited by Richard Labonté. Selected and
introduced by Larry Duplechan.
ISBN 978-1-57344-753-9, $15.95

Best Gay Erotica 2011
Edited by Richard Labonté.
Selected and introduced by Kevin Killian.
ISBN 978-1-57344-424-8 $15.95

Best Gay Erotica 2010
Edited by Richard Labonté. Selected and
introduced by Blair Mastbaum.
ISBN 978-1-57344-374-6 $15.95

In Sleeping Beauty's Bed
Erotic Fairy Tales
By Mitzi Szereto
ISBN 978-1-57344-367-8 $16.95

Can't Help the Way That I Feel
Sultry Stories of African American Love
Edited by Lori Bryant-Woolridge
ISBN 978-1-57344-386-9 $14.95

Making the Hook-Up
Edgy Sex with Soul
Edited by Cole Riley
ISBN 978-1-57344-3838 $14.95

* **Free book of equal or lesser value. Shipping and applicable sales tax extra.**
Cleis Press • (800) 780-2279 • orders@cleispress.com
www.cleispress.com

Ordering is easy! Call us toll free or fax us to place your MC/VISA order.
You can also mail the order form below with payment to:
Cleis Press, 2246 Sixth St., Berkeley, CA 94710.

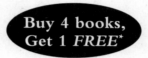

ORDER FORM

QTY	TITLE	PRICE
_____	_____	_____
_____	_____	_____
_____	_____	_____
_____	_____	_____
_____	_____	_____
_____	_____	_____
_____	_____	_____
_____	_____	_____

	SUBTOTAL	_____
	SHIPPING	_____
	SALES TAX	_____
	TOTAL	_____

Add $3.95 postage/handling for the first book ordered and $1.00 for each additional book. Outside North America, please contact us for shipping rates. California residents add 8.75% sales tax. Payment in U.S. dollars only.

* Free book of equal or lesser value. Shipping and applicable sales tax extra.

Cleis Press • Phone: (800) 780-2279 • Fax: (510) 845-8001
orders@cleispress.com • www.cleispress.com
You'll find more great books on our website

Follow us on Twitter @cleispress • Friend/fan us on Facebook